If Only for ANOTHER Night

Jaylin Rogers
Brenda Hampton, Contributor

VOICES BOOKS & PUBLISHING

PUBLISHER'S NOTE

This book is a work of fiction. Names, characters, places and incidents either are the product of the author's imagination or are used fictitiously, and any resemblances to actual persons, living or dead, business establishments, events or locales is entirely coincidental.

ISBN: 978-1500123178

Special thanks to all of the READERS who also make great WRITERS!

Giana Monroe
Dhi'Mon Hines
Ashley Benton
Shelia B.
Myra Walker
Kalima Shahada
Tiffani Warren
Veronique
Author Known

BACK DOWN MEMORY LANE
Author Unknown

I heard that traveling back down memory lane wasn't the best thing to do, but when it came to Jaylin, I was willing to consider the risk. Today was his birthday, and for the past several weeks, we'd been conversing over the phone, more than usual. He'd been sending me text messages that made me a little hot and bothered, and on the hush-hush, I'd been sending him some that had him eager to *see* me too. Now that he was single again, and my current relationship was on the rocks, I figured that we could do no harm by hooking up—*If Only for Another Night*. That was all I needed to satisfy the growing urge I had for him, and as I prepared for his arrival, I couldn't stop thinking about the numerous orgasms I suspected were coming my way.

Whenever Jaylin came to St. Louis, normally, he'd stay at a hotel, or he'd stay at a condo in Weldon Spring he helped me purchase about a year ago. We had that kind of relationship, and the way I looked at it, we were way more than just occasional lovers. We were good friends—friends who could always depend on each other for just about anything. We weren't trying to fall in love, wasn't interested in pursuing a serious relationship, and we were at a point where there was nothing that either of us could do anymore to hurt each other. He didn't give two cents about who I dated, and quite frankly, the countless loves of his life didn't disturb me either. Pertaining to a serious relationship, we'd been there, done that before, and would never attempt to go there again. More than anything, we grew to understand each other. He was more difficult to understand than I was, but as the years trickled by, I began to focus more on the things about him that intrigued me, rather than the things about him that disappointed me, or should I say, the things I couldn't change. That was how I managed to be at peace with him, but the truth was, not every woman was capable of ignoring some of his interesting ways.

With that being said, I had to admit that many things about Jaylin changed after his divorce from Nokea. I predicted that he would never do right by any woman, but I still knew in my heart that he loved Nokea as best as he could. I also knew that his love elevated to the highest level that it could reach would never satisfy her. Simply because the love he had for himself . . . his needs and his wants, superseded everything and everyone. That was a fact.

As the sun went down, I glanced at the clock on the wall. Jaylin was supposed to arrive at seven o'clock, but he was late. I was kind of surprised, because he had a reputation for always being prompt. He'd curse out a person for being late, so his tardiness alluded to the fact that something could've been wrong. I reached for my cellphone to call him, but then I decided against it. I didn't want him to think that I was eager to see him, even though I was. We had a potential movie deal to discuss, and I also wanted to find out what had really been going on in his world. During some of our more recent conversations over the phone, he seemed happy. Business had been booming and money was flowing like rain. He also mentioned that he hadn't been sexually satisfied in a very long time, but that was because, according to him, he hadn't made time to indulge himself. Money had become his priority, and it was the one thing he loved more than pussy.

I paced the floor in my bedroom with my thoughts locked on Jaylin. A few months had gone by since I'd last seen him, and the last time he was here, things didn't go so well. His mood was off. Every time I asked a question he snapped at me. I inquired about Nokea and Scorpio, but he acted as if it was a crime for me to mention their names. So, I backed off and let him talk about what was going on when he was ready to.

I tidied my room a little then my eyes shifted to the clock again. It was almost eight o'clock. Instead of calling him, I went into the bathroom to check myself in the mirror. My brown, tinted hair was full of bouncing and behaving curls that fell a few inches past my shoulders. Very little makeup covered my light skin, but the nude color lip gloss I wore made my lips appear fuller. Since sex was, most likely, on the agenda tonight, I accented my healthy curves with a black, sheer and silk negligee that revealed my meaty breasts and coochie that used to have Jaylin's mark on it. I sprayed several dashes of sweet perfume over my body, and then picked up a can of hairspray. Right then, the alarm chimed and alerted me that someone had entered through the front door. I hurried to put the hairspray down, and then stepped into the five-inch stilettos that were on the floor near my bed. My silk, thigh-high robe was nearby, so I put it on. It stayed slightly open, just so Jaylin could get a peek of what he hadn't tasted in quite some time. There was no secret that we both had been kind of stingy with the goods, but it was always a pleasure to make up for lost time.

As I sauntered down the narrow hallway, my heels sounded off on the hardwood floor. The second I reached the foyer, I halted my steps. Jaylin stood, fumbling through a stack of his mail I always left on the table for him. His head was lowered, but I could see the sharp lining around his curly, healthy hair. His goatee was suited well around his mouth and chin, and his smooth light skin glistened with a tan. The aroma of Clive Christian cologne infused the entire foyer, and he rocked a navy, V-neck cashmere sweater that melted on his muscles. I glanced down at his shoes, and the bottom of his dark blue jeans hung slightly over his shiny leather loafers. The bulge in his jeans was in full effect, as was the blinding Rolex with diamonds that adorned his wrist. Like always, he was clean cut, clean shaven and polished to perfection. I assumed that he'd heard my footsteps, but he remained occupied with the mail. As he began to open a letter, he looked up. His luring gray eyes slowly traveled from the top of my head to the tips of my stilettos. He didn't blink, didn't smile, didn't smirk and didn't speak. Neither did I. Eventually, he was the one to break the utter silence.

"What's up, Miss Author?" he said.

I strutted forward while tightening the belt on my robe to hide my goodies. "What's up is you. I thought you weren't going to say anything, and how rude is that, especially when you enter someone's home?"

"It's not rude for a man not to speak when he enters a residence that has his name on it, is it? And the last time I checked, I have more ownership of this place than you do. Besides that, it's my birthday. You're the one who should be speaking up and going all out for me."

"I agree. And as soon as you taste the triple layer, red velvet cake that I made for you, you'll see how much I went all out for you. I mean, I went waaay out there. Almost to hell and back."

He wet his bottom lip with his tongue and nodded. "Red velvet cake, huh? While I always appreciate your efforts, I'm sure it tastes nothing like the one Nanny B made for me."

"If it doesn't, then please take that up with the Cheesecake Factory. They're the ones you should or shouldn't give all the credit to. All I had to do was drive there to go get it."

"Yeah, that's what I thought."

Jaylin lowered his head and started to read the letter in his hand. Like always, he was unpredictable. I couldn't tell what kind of mood he was in, and for it to be his birthday, I expected for him to be a bit more hyped. Being nosy, I moved closer to him, trying to peek at the letter.

"What's that?" I asked. "A disconnection notice?"

He cocked his head back then closed the letter so I wouldn't read it. "Damn, why you all up in my business? And the only thing I'm going to disconnect is you."

I playfully shivered and hit him with some straight truth. "You wish you could disconnect me. But whenever you're ready to, just let me know. As for the letter, since you have some of your stuff mailed here, I have access to it. If I really wanted to read it, I would have opened it and glued it back together like I did your bank statements. But I remember how upset you got about me looking at your statements, so I decided not to open the letter."

"Don't remind me," he said then laid his mail on the table. "And keep in mind that I have access to a whole lot of your *stuff* too."

The direction of his eyes traveled to the vicinity of my pussy. I knew where he was going with his comment, and it would be wrong for me to deny the truth. Instead, I followed behind him as he smooth walked his way to the kitchen. He opened the fridge and complained about it being empty.

"I swear, a man don't get no love on his birthday. If you knew I was coming, you could've gone to the grocery store. I guess we're going to be eating ham sandwiches and chips for the next few days, huh?"

"Unfortunately, I don't cook for men who have high demands. And just in case you didn't notice, there is a McDonald's, Jack-in-the-Box, and KFC around the corner. You should've stopped, but since you didn't, there is an ice-cold beer in the fridge and some leftover lasagna in the freezer. The cake that I'm sure you'll enjoy is over there on the counter."

Jaylin removed a cold bottle of Bud Light from the fridge then closed it. He walked over to the counter and observed the cake.

"Looks good, but there's too much icing on top. Must be, at least, an inch on there, ain't it?"

I went over to the counter and swiped my finger on top of the cake. A healthy portion of cream cheese frosting covered my finger. I lifted it close to Jaylin's lips and smiled. "Maybe not an inch, but I'm not one to complain about inches. You shouldn't either."

He wet his lips again, and then lifted his hand to hold my finger. His sexy eyes shifted to my breasts then back to the icing on my finger. Without saying a word, he opened his mouth and used the tip of his curled tongue to lick most of the icing from my finger. We stared at each other without a blink, and when the icing was all gone, I pulled my finger away.

"Delicious," Jaylin said in a soft tone. "Almost as good as you."

Before I could respond, he walked away to the hearth room. While sitting on the couch, he held the beer in his hand and propped his feet on the leather ottoman in front of him. I straddled the bottom section of his legs and sat on top of them. My butt was on his legs and the ottoman, so he couldn't move. He narrowed his eyes to gaze between my legs, but all he could see was the sheer crotch section that covered my shaved coochie lips.

"Now that I have your attention," I said. "You never mentioned why you were late."

His eyes widened as he looked up at me. "Got tied up at the rental car check-in. The man in front of me didn't have his shit together, so I had to wait. And why are you asking about my lateness? Were you looking forward to seeing me? I guess so, since your pussy speaks louder than words."

"It's a good thing that my pussy doesn't speak for me. I thought I did."

"Not today you don't. Besides, when it comes to us, you lie a lot. I can always count on your pussy to tell me what's up, when I see it cream filled."

"It's not quite there yet, sorry."

"No need to apologize, especially when I have such a clear view of things from where I'm sitting. Trust me when I say you're there, baby. I can always tell when you miss me."

I blushed and leaned back on hands. My legs fell further apart, just so I could share my pussy's inner thoughts. "Of course *we* miss you, Jaylin, but I understand that you're such a busy man who doesn't have much time to entertain anymore. That's why I made sure the spare room was nice and comfy for you, just in case you require space and prefer to be alone on your birthday."

For the first time tonight, he smiled. He stared at me then picked up the beer bottle. He positioned it close to his lips then slipped his tongue into the hole, before taking a sip. Afterwards, he cleared his throat.

"I always make time to entertain, but the truth is, I've gotten kind of bored with certain things, or should I say, with certain individuals from my past. How dare anybody believe that the grass would be greener on the other side? I've had the pleasure of rejecting certain people, as they now realize the green grass on the other side turned out to be more like muddy waters."

He was so good at talking in circles, so I pushed for a little more clarification. "When you speak of people from your past who believe the grass is greener on the other side, I suspect you're talking about Nokea and Scorpio. If you are, I wouldn't necessarily say they're in your past, only because you do see them almost every day, don't you?"

"See, I most certainly do. Touch, I do not or have not, until I get ready to. While we all remain great parents, my life now revolves around more than two women who are living with regrets."

Jaylin was a mess. He acted as if he didn't want to elaborate on this subject, but the truth was he did. Maybe after a few more of those beers, and several shots of Remy, he would be willing to spill his guts.

"Speaking of regrets," I said. "That includes you too, doesn't it? And what did Nokea and Scorpio get you for your birthday?"

"I have some regrets, but it still doesn't change the fact that I'm leaving the past behind. Washing my hands to it all, baby, and I'm feeling good about finally living my life for me and only me. For my birthday, they gave me exactly what I wanted—love, peace and respect. Now, if you don't mind, I'd like to change the subject. Give me the scoop on what's been happening in your world. You said there's been a lot going on, so let me hear it."

Hell, he'd been living his life the way he wanted to all along, and certainly didn't need a wake-up call from me. I could sense a slight attitude from him, but he was the one who decided to mention women in his past. Whether he was willing to admit his mistakes or not, Nokea was the only woman capable of bringing out the best in him. I had witnessed that much over the years, and none of the women he'd been with, including me, could ever deny or compete with the feelings he had for her. There was nothing we could do to tamper with his heart, but tampering with his dick was now an option.

"In my world," I said. "I'm trying to make some interesting things happen. But before I do anything, I need for you to sign this contract, relinquishing all of your rights to films, books, DVD's, etc. A while back you stated that you didn't want to be included in any of this. I want to be sure that what you said still stands."

Jaylin asked to see the contract, so I got up to go get it. I placed it on his lap then sat next to him on the couch. While he read the contract, I remained silent. He was so serious when it came to business, and pertaining to our previous contract regarding these matters, every "i" had been dotted and "t" had been crossed. That all changed, however, when the truth about his character being real was revealed on Facebook, and in the novel, *In My Shoes.*

"While you're reading that over," I said. "Can I tell you what some of the readers have been saying about you?"

With his eyes glued to the contract, he softly rubbed his goatee and nodded.

"Some women are mad at you because they say that you don't like voluptuous women. Others are upset because you no longer reply to your emails, and a few women are downright sick and tired of you. They didn't approve of your snobby ways in *Hell House*, and then there are plenty, along with the Naughty Angels, who miss you dearly. They want some Jay-Baby time. I'm kind of onboard with them too."

Jaylin didn't respond until he was done reading the contract. He placed it on the table then turned to address me. "The majority of black men who I know, love and appreciate women with meat on their bones. I am no exception. And there ain't shit I can do about people who are sick and tired of me—it be that way sometimes. Just know that some of those same people will be the first to read an upcoming book with me as the character. I'll be the first to admit that I'm very hard to live with, *Hell House* or no *Hell House*, so what did they expect? And I ain't got nothing but love for the people who get me and understand where I'm coming from. Pertaining to the Naughty Angels, they all know that we share a lifetime bond. That situation is all good, and if my time is required, all they need to do is ask. That goes for you as well. Have I ever denied you my time?"

I sat there, pretending to be in thought. Yes, he had denied me his time, but I didn't want to go down a list of his faults because we needed to get back to the specifics in the contract. Since I didn't respond, Jaylin got on his knees and positioned his body in between my legs. He scooted me down and leaned in so close that I could feel what he was packing. With a serious look washed across his face, he questioned me again.

"Have I ever, Miss Author, denied you my time?"

My heart started to beat a little faster. With his dick pressing against my hotspot, I had to come correct.

"Yes," I replied.

"When?"

"So many times that I can't remember. But that was then and this is now. Now, I need for you to tell me what you think of the contract and sign it."

He squeezed my thighs then planted a soft kiss at the center of my forehead. "I don't sign contracts without my attorney looking things over first. You already know that, so why play games with me?"

"No games, just business."

"Business doesn't come with a black negligee on, hard nipples and a warm and wet pussy. Only you do."

I shrugged. "Ignore what you see and tell me how you really feel."

"Glad you asked, so here it goes. The next time my birthday comes around, leave the negligee in the closet. That shit is a waste of money and time, because I don't care how well you dress that pussy up for me, it will still taste the same, feel the same and operate the same way for me, when my dick or tongue enters it. Now, go take that shit off and meet me in my room, not yours, in five minutes."

He definitely had a point about the feel and taste of it, but I always . . . always had a problem with Jaylin being in control of things. I wanted to fuck his brains out tonight, and even though I had put sex on the agenda, I decided to . . . wait. I did, however, enjoy the feel of his bulge growing between my legs, so in the moment, I reached up and ran my fingers through the back of his soft hair.

"Next time, I will leave the negligee in the closet, but meanwhile, I have a simple question for you. You keep talking about moving away from individuals in your past. I assume that includes me. But then here you are, trying to get your fuck on, *If Only for Another Night*."

The smirk on Jaylin's face said it all. He was always up to no good, but I sensed it from the beginning. "A man must get some kind of pleasure on his birthday, and I couldn't think of anyone else I would rather get down and dirty with than you. But after tonight, baby, it's a done deal."

This motherfucker was smooth . . . too smooth. He backed away from me and stood to remove his sweater. That damn muscle-packed body of his was cut in all the right places, and as he unlatched his belt buckle, his jeans lowered by several inches. I looked directly at his eyes, trying my best to ignore all of the goodness that stood before me. Looking into his eyes was no better, but for now they kept me focused. I stared deep into them and smiled.

"I had major plans to get down and dirty with you tonight too, Jaylin, but you seem to think that the way to a woman's heart starts by traveling between her legs. I've listened to—"

He halted my words when he reached for my hand and pulled me up from the couch. He eased his arms around my waist and held my body close to his. I took a deep breath, causing my breasts to rise against his chest. His scent got to me; I damn near melted in his arms.

"No, I never said that the way to a woman's heart was by going between her legs, and if I did, I don't think that way anymore. What I believe is the way to a real woman's heart is by traveling through her strong mind. But you already know that I'm not interested in capturing hearts anymore. What I'm interested in tonight is some hardcore sex that can keep me entertained for hours. As I mentioned to you during our conversations, I haven't been there in a while. Haven't had sex with nobody . . . not one single woman in almost six months, because I wanted to take some time away from all of the shit that transpired in my life and reflect on some things. Money has been my focus, but the truth is, I still get lonely too. I still fantasize about being in that pussy, but timing is everything. So, either you're with me tonight or you're not. If not, say the word so I can take my cake and jet."

Jaylin waited for me to respond, but I couldn't. This was hard because I had been there to witness everything he had been through. I didn't want to reject him, and I also didn't want to deprive myself of a night of pure pleasure, that only he could deliver. Since I hadn't said a word, he released his arms from around me. He gave me a quick kiss on the cheek then backed away.

"I'm going to a hotel," he said with his brows arched inward, showing a hint of frustration with me. "And I'll get back to you about that contract, as soon as I can."

He tossed his sweater over his shoulder and swiped up the contract from the table. I stood, pondering my next move. By the time that move was made, he was already near the front door. I called out to him, and he turned to face me while standing in the foyer.

"You already know how I feel about you, but maybe it is time for you to experience some different women. Maybe someone else can offer you what the women from your past couldn't, or maybe you will discover that being alone is simply okay. That'll be for you decide. Keep me posted on how it goes, and whatever you do, please don't hurt nobody, okay?"

Thankfully, he displayed a tiny smile. "That's all I've been trying to say, but you act like you took offense to it, more so, like you wasn't trying to hear me. I need a change, but I can't promise you that I won't hurt nobody down the road. I'll think about keeping you posted, but in the meantime, be good, sweetheart. I'll be back, and you already know why."

"Yes, I do. Because Y.D.K.L.L.Y.K.L.W.M."

"Exactly," he said then pounded his chest. "And that's between us."

Yes it was. He was right at the door when I realized that he was leaving without his cake, but that was the last thing on my mind. When he touched the doorknob, I rushed up from behind and called his name again. He turned with a puzzled look on his face.

"One more thing," I said. "I forgot something."

I wrapped my arms around his neck, and pursued an intense lip-lock with him that caused both of our hands to roam. The second he tried to slip his thick fingers inside of me, I grabbed his hand and backed away.

"Okay," he said. "I'm out. But with a pussy releasing that much heat, I know you're still in my corner."

I released his hand. "Always, Jaylin. Through the thick and thin, highs and lows, ups and downs . . . I'm here. Ready to share all of your business with the world."

He snickered, winked at me then shook his head. After shutting the door behind him, I wondered if he realized that I was telling the truth!

SHOW ME WHAT YOU GOT

Dhi'Mon Hines

I will never in my life forget the day I met Jaylin Rogers. It was and still is the most exhilarating, mind-blowing and heart-pumping experience of my life. I had just gotten a job at my first public relations firm since getting my bachelor's degree and I decided to take a celebratory vacation.

Seeing how I had never been, I couldn't think of anyplace else to go for a quick vacation but to the hot city of Miami, Florida. By "quick" I meant one night and I was out the next morning. My first day working would be in two days, so a day-cation was all I could manage.

Stepping off of the plane, I stood with my bottled water, feeling the sun beat down on my face. It was seven o'clock in the morning and eighty-nine degrees outside. Good thing I had opted to wear a crop top and shorts. Normally, wearing my legs out was something I chose not to do, but after checking the weather yesterday I knew little clothing was needed.

"The sun just came up and it's already hot as hell out here!" My best friend, Marisha, complained while standing behind me. Marisha was my outspoken best friend of ten years, so naturally, she had to come with me to Miami. "Can we please go find some AC before I turn into a damn puddle?"

"Yeah, girl, let's go. We need to go check into the hotel anyway and start the day. Our only day here."

"Yassss! Now, that's better!"

After trying on outfits for about two-and-a-half hours, I finally felt satisfied with my outfit for the night. My black lace cocktail dress finally looked good on me, after being tried on about five times. For years, I had this habit of hating everything I put on. There was always something about what I put on that made me look funny, in my eyes.

While standing in front of the mirror, I examined my outfit. The dress looked very sexy on me. It made my small 5'7 frame look curvy and accentuated my perky B-cup breasts and small, but firm, ass. The nude, sling-back Steve Maddens I wore gave me extra height and complimented my soft, caramel legs. My wavy-top bun showed off my round face and the red, MAC lipstick made my freckles and natural red hair POP!

"If you don't bring your ass!" Marisha shouted.

She had been yelling at me for the past two hours to hurry up and get dressed. Although she was used to me taking forever to get dressed, she was just as anxious as I was to get out and about.

I walked out the door, while singing along with Lauryn Hill's song playing on my phone: "Ready or not, here I come. You can't hide . . ."

"Ready or not, bitch, I'm leaving!" Marisha scolded me as she walked out the room with me, following close behind. "Doesn't make any damn sense for you to take that long!"

"Stop acting like this is something new! At least it didn't take me four hours, like when we went to that Trey Songz concert." Shaking my head at the memory, I was ashamed just saying that.

"Trust, if you would have tried to pull that stunt again, you would definitely have been left!"

"Yeah, yeah, yeah! I hear you talking. You look real cute by the way."

She had on a red, double-slit maxi dress and black Steve Madden pumps. The double slit showed off her long brown legs that were the envy of many women, including myself.

"I know I look bad, and it didn't take me three hours to look this good either!" she shot at me.

I threw her a quick side eye then stepped into the hotel's elevator. We were headed to Club LIV. We'd gone to the Miami Heat game earlier and Marisha was told LIV was a Miami hotspot by some guy she'd met.

It didn't hurt that it was a five-minute walk from our hotel either. The money we'd save off not having to take a cab would buy us some extra drinks tonight.

Walking through the doors of the Fontainebleau Hotel, I had a very 'You're Not In Kansas Anymore' moment. It was beautiful. There were black and white marble floors, champagne colored chandeliers, with an elegant chaise lounge. Everything looked so exotic. My next trip to Miami, I will definitely make it a point to stay in one of the rooms, at least, for a night.

As we rounded the corner of the front entrance to the club, we saw men and women standing in a line.

"This cannot be the line!" I gasped, feeling agitation come over me. People were standing everywhere, attempting to get inside the club. Some were even waving money in the air.

A Hispanic lady with long hair and wide hips turned toward us, "Yes, Chica, it is the line. May as well take those heels off and step to the back. Get comfortable, because you'll be standing for a while."

Looking around, I could tell this was going to be one of those nights to piss me off. Marisha tapped my shoulder and pointed in the direction of one of the bouncers. His hand was up, as if he was summoning her over. He looked familiar, but I couldn't put my finger on where I'd seen his face.

We started toward him, and as we got closer to him, I finally remembered the familiar face. It was the guy from the Heat game that Marisha had been talking to. He looked way more handsome than I remembered him being. He was tall, dark brown, with a muscular build. The black suit he wore gave him a businesslike look. The man cleaned up very well.

"Did he look like that earlier?" I asked Marisha as we walked toward him.

"Yes, he did. You just ain't notice 'cause you like your men light as a yellow crayon," she whispered. Marisha was an advocate for the dark chocolate fellas.

"No, I like them handsome and clean with something big swangin' down between their . . ." Marisha nudged my side to shut me up and we both laughed.

After standing at the door for five minutes of Marisha and the bouncer talking and making "I wanna freak you" eyes at each other, we finally entered the club. Soon as we strutted in, my mouth opened wide. The club was just as exotic looking as the lobby of the hotel it was in. Being from North Carolina, seeing clubs like this was a rarity.

Purple and blue lights graced the walls. It was structured like the inside of a palace. Everything from the lounges, to the staircases, to the superdome resembling roof, it all came together in a majestic way. It was crowded with people. The DJ was playing Wale's song "That Way" overhead and people were talking, drinking, and dancing all over the place.

"Damn, I see why getting in is hard!" I yelled to Marisha who finally stopped looking back at the bouncer who was eyeing her body down like she was a homemade scoop of ice cream. She was switching so hard, I thought her hip would pop out of place.

"You ain't lying! This place is decked completely out!" She yelled back at me. "That is going to be the father of my future chocolate kids." She nudged her head toward the bouncer. "Looking like a dark chocolate Hershey bar."

We both burst into a fit of laughs. "You eye fucked him so hard that you're probably pregnant with one of those chocolate kids right now!"

She agreed and we made our way over to the bar. It was overcrowded, so we decided to find someplace else to sit. There were lounge areas placed throughout the club. From a short distance, all of them looked filled up. Then, we noticed an open lounge of seats near the bar area that sat somewhat secluded from the others. Before someone else could get to it, we rushed to grab the seats. It wasn't as loud in the lounge, as it seemed to be everywhere else in the club. While at our seats, I noticed there was a drink with what appeared to be dark liquor in it on a table that sat in front of one of the lounge seats. A waitress walked up and asked for our drink orders. After we ordered, she told us she'd be back with our drinks. As the waitress got near the bar, I saw her being halted by a man. Trying to be discreetly nosy, I leaned forward, attempting to see who stopped her. Her body was blocking my view of the man. Eventually, I gave up on seeing who he was, but continued to observe the waitress from the corner of my eye.

By watching her body language, it seemed as though she was apologizing for something. I assumed it had something to do with us. Once they finished the heated conversation, I saw her walking back toward us with him close behind.

She stopped in front of us and my suspicions were confirmed, "I'm sorry, but these seats were supposed to be reserved for someone else. I apologize for the inconvenience, but if you'd like to follow me, I will find you two seats in another lounge area."

Although I was a bit irritated by us having to move, especially after getting comfortable, it was not a situation that would ruin my night.

"That's fine." I stood to walk off with the waitress. Marisha, however, wasn't having it. She didn't budge, and as I walked off, I could hear her yelling.

"Oh, hell no! This is not fine with me! There is plenty of room for us all to sit here. I'm comfortable and I'm not moving! What motherfucker is so big that they can't share pretty much an entire section of a club? If it ain't Rick Ross then the answer is NOBODY."

I was too embarrassed to turn around and see what was going on. All I heard was the man, with much hostility in his voice, yell too. "I'm the too big motherfucker that does not and will not be sharing my reserved section of this club! Now, the lady asked you nicely to move. Me . . . I will not be so nice."

Marisha's voice got louder. "And who in the hell are you supposed to be?"

Just then, I turned around and took several steps toward her, as soon as the man with much pride in his voice said, "I am Jaylin Rogers. And you're about to be one extremely embarrassed woman, if you do not vacate from my section. This is my last and final warning."

All of a sudden, my heart felt as if it had stopped beating. You would have thought somebody had told me Tupac was alive and doing a concert. There was no way I had heard him correctly. I stood with a dumbfounded look plastered across my face. Maybe I should have grabbed Marisha and just left, since I was probably looking dumb as hell. But moving was not an option, because at the moment, I felt as if I was having an out-of-body experience. I couldn't believe it was him!

After Jaylin's last warning, I assumed Marisha had finally gotten the hint. She stood, while sucking her teeth and flipping him off. "Come on, girl." She grabbed my arm. "Let's get the hell away from here."

As I'd said before, I could not move, let alone walk. When she grabbed me, I stumbled and damn near fell flat on my face, right in front of Jaylin.

"Whoa!" he said. With quickness, he scooped me by my waist and pulled me close to his buffed chest to hold me. Trying to steady me and give me a chance to walk straight, he released my waist then backed away from me.

Either the fall had me flustered or the fact that the man with his body pressed against mine was the man of my every fantasy for the past three or four years. Whichever it was, all I knew was that once I tried to walk again, my knees buckled. Yet again, he caught me. This time, he did not release me from his grip.

"Listen," he whispered into my ear with what sounded like that of a Greek God mixed with the sound of angels. "I need you to be still for a moment. You're trying to move too fast and you seem to be a little, or a lot, intoxicated." Little did he know, I was overly intoxicated, but it was not from alcohol.

We stood for a moment with his arm still wrapped around my waist. As I started to regain my composure and bring my thoughts together, I knew I had to get out of this space with him. I tried to steady myself, but as I moved my body, he pressed a bit harder. That's when I felt his manhood jump. Had I not been pressed against his body, I would have sworn somebody had grabbed a damn snake and put it up my dress.

When his dick flexed again, I jumped and stumbled two steps backwards. Our eyes connected, and I couldn't help but notice the amused expression on his face. Suddenly, embarrassment spread over me. I didn't know what in the hell was wrong with me? He had me completely out of my element. So much so that I ignored every word Marisha was saying in the background. It all sounded like mumbo jumbo to me. My eyes were glued to Jaylin, and I checked him out, as he stood strong and tall, with a stance exuding nothing but confidence and power. His face was smooth shaven and his goatee was lined to perfection. He had perfect jet black natural curls. The hint of a smile displayed on his mouth showed his smooth, supple lips and pearly white teeth. The crisp white button-down shirt he wore could barely contain his muscular build. I could see myself ripping that shirt to shreds and licking him all over. I was seriously in a trance, and trying to avoid eye contact, I finally found my voice.

"Thank you. I apologize for my friend and me. We didn't mean to take your area nor did I mean to invade your privacy like that."

Marisha was still on edge. "Do not apologize to him! He could have shared those seats, especially since he was over here feeling you up!"

In my head, I started to wish I had left her ass at home and came to Miami alone. "Girl, chill out," I hissed at her while willing her with my eyes to shut the hell up.

Her eyebrows shot up, showing me she had gotten the hint. "Whatever. Speak for yourself with the apology. I'm going to check if my boo went on break. Come find me when you're finished with his arrogant ass." She walked off and Jaylin yelled after her.

"Thank you for the compliment. I get that a lot!"

She shot him her middle finger, but he chuckled and shook his head.

I wanted to laugh too, but I found myself in a situation where I had to apologize for Marisha again. "Sorry for the finger gestures too. She didn't mean that. She was just upset that we had to move." I took a hard swallow, and then looked in another direction to avoid eye contact with him. I didn't know why I felt so damn shy around him. He made me feel like I was some fourteen-year-old girl crushing on a boy.

He spoke in a smooth, sexy voice. "No need to apologize. She meant exactly what she said. Plus, it's not the first time I've been called an arrogant ass. No harm done."

"That is so true!" The words fell out of my mouth before I could even think about it. His eyebrows had shot up. "Shit! I mean, I'm sorry. I wasn't . . . I just . . . ugh. Forgive me, because I'm a mess right now. I . . . I," I stammered. He stepped a little closer to me. He was close enough that I could smell the panty-dropping cologne he was wearing.

Whatever he had on complimented him well. Maybe I inhaled too deeply because I swayed a little. This time, he reached for my arm and asked me to sit. I didn't know what it was he was doing to me, but it sure took a toll on my entire body.

He sat me down and excused himself. I watched as he casually walked up to a waitress and started speaking to her.

The blush that spread across her face made me laugh to myself. She was flustered just as I was by him.

I quickly looked down as he turned to walk back over to me. I was relieved when he sat in front of me, rather than beside me. Another whiff of him, I was sure to faint.

"The waitress will be over soon to bring you a glass of water. What's your name?" He said with concern slightly etched on his face.

"Dhi'Mon." I responded, but didn't dare to lift my head to look at him.

"Like the gem?"

"I guess. Not so much spelled the same." I was pleased that he didn't ask, "Like *The Players Club*?" I'd been asked that one too many times.

"Well, Ms. Dhi'Mon. For the record, why don't you tell me how much you had to drink? From your actions, obviously a lot."

I sighed and spilled the truth, "I haven't had anything to drink."

"Nothing?" he questioned again.

With my head still lowered and shyness plastered on my face, I shook my head. This was so unlike me. I didn't fawn over guys. Normally, I showed them who was boss. Me.

Catching me off guard, Jaylin reached across the table and lifted my chin with his finger. My eyes locked with his. My body felt as though it had burst into a thousand and one flames. His eyes were hypnotizing. Just one look into them and he could charm the panties off of any woman. It was as if he was the male Medusa. But instead of turning me into stone, he turned me into a woman in heat. I regretted not wearing panties. I squeezed my thighs together tightly, as the rush of my wetness started to flow. I crossed my legs and rubbed my thighs to cool off. Jaylin gazed at me, as if he knew my insides were filled with moisture.

"You sure you're not drunk?" he asked with a sly smirk on his face.

Again, I answered honestly. "Unfortunately, no." It was unfortunate because, if I were drunk, I'd have an excuse for acting like a nervous fool.

It seemed like forever before the waitress came and sat down the cup of water Jaylin had asked for. In reality, it may have only been sixty seconds, because we'd been sitting there just staring at each other while in deep thought. Ever since coming in contact with his addictive eyes, I couldn't stop looking into them. They were intoxicating—He was intoxicating.

"Damn, I'm being rude." He extended his hand to me. "I'm Jaylin."

I chuckled under my breath. It was really him. "I know," I said in response. "I know all about you, Mr. Rogers."

He looked at me with a puzzled expression. "You know me?" He leaned back with his arms crossed. "Tell me . . . how is it that you know me, Miss Dhi'Mon?"

A laugh escaped my lips. I gazed at his lips then nodded. "Yeah. I guess you can say that I know you. A lot."

He softly stroked his goatee as though he was trying to figure out where I knew him from. "Care to elaborate?"

Now that I was sitting and not pressed up against his body, I felt confident enough to talk to him. "Well, I'm an avid reader and you just so happen to be the subject of one of my favorite author's books."

Within seconds, the inquisitive expression on his face turned into a smile. He grinned like a schoolboy, he was so sexy. Looking at him made me hot, so I picked up my water to take a sip. Though I already had an idea of how amazing he looked, it was nothing like seeing him in the flesh.

Just for a second, he seemed a little tense. He began to roll up his sleeves, and curious about the look on his face, I asked if he'd had a rough day. Before answering, he reached for the drink that had been sitting on the table and took a quick swallow. Afterwards, he sat the glass back down.

"I guess you can say that my day has been a little rough," he said. "I may need to get out of here and go somewhere to relax."

I wanted to do the same, but I questioned him further about his rough day. "Would your rough day have anything to do with Nokea or Scorpio?"

He shot me a blank stare, along with a dirty look that dared me not to go there with him.

I took heed and just shook my head. I'd read all of the books in Brenda Hampton's Naughty Series, so I knew that he had his hands full with women problems. Curiosity got the best of me so I had to ask, "What are you doing here? Are you meeting someone? I don't want to intrude."

He looked at me with a raised eyebrow. Before he could say anything, I let him know I wasn't trying to pry or be nosy.

"No one intrudes in my life, unless I want them to. And if I have a feeling that they're being too nosy, I would tell that person to mind their business. I'm not getting that from you, so feel free to hit me with any question that you would like to." He responded with virtually zero humor in his voice.

Something was obviously bothering him, so I just sat back and shrugged. He smirked, "To answer your prior questions, I just needed some time to have a drink and sit back without anyone bothering me."

I countered, "In a club?"

He shrugged. "I can't think of a better place."

"Okay, your prerogative." I smiled at him, attempting to lighten the mood. I'd dreamed of the day I'd sit in front of this man and ask him some personal questions. I hoped that he would be willing and able to go there with me. I pondered on what to say.

"Why do you treat women the way you do? Why can't you be faithful to Nokea or to anyone else for that matter? Why this?

Why that?" Then I'd curse him out for treating women the way he does. But for some reason, I couldn't bring myself to do any of that. Being in his presence told me he was a different kind of man.

Instead of questioning him, I just sat there marveling at the fact that I was sitting in front of Jaylin Jerome Rogers. For now. Eventually, I expected for my curiosity to get the best of me.

"Uh um!" Someone cleared their throat. I looked up to see Marisha standing with the bouncer. She rolled her eyes at Jaylin and he smiled at her. "Dhi'Mon, I'm about to leave with Andre."

"Who?" I questioned her with a screwed face.

"An-Dre," she said, nudging her head in his direction with every syllable.

"Ohhh! Andre." I giggled.

"Yeah, girl, so are you coming? He can drop you off at the hotel or are you going to take a taxi back? It's only a five-minute walk, but I really don't want you walking alone." She spoke with concern on her face and a tinge of irritation. I'm guessing because Jaylin was present.

"I'm a big girl. I'll get back on my own. Check out at the hotel is at one o'clock, so please come back by then." I reminded her with a smile and a wink.

"Okay, mom. I'll be back by curfew," she said in a joking manner. We air kissed each other's cheeks, and Marisha walked off with the bouncer. She halted her steps, just to hiss another "arrogant ass" at Jaylin.

"How many times do you want me to agree with you? Now, go handle your business, and allow me to handle mine," Jaylin said. Marisha rolled her eyes and walked off. He then looked at me. "Your friend is a character."

"Yes, she definitely is. I'm surprised by your reaction though. Earlier, it seemed you were a bit uptight."

"That's because it's been a long day for me. But as for you, you seemed a little intoxicated earlier. Why is that, if you haven't had any alcohol?"

I knew what he was getting at, but I played it off. "If you haven't noticed, I'm very bowlegged. That can make me a tad bit clumsy."

"Oh, I definitely noticed just how bowlegged you are. That's a plus for me."

He seduced me with his eyes, as they roamed my body. It felt as though he was looking right through me. He was assessing me, as I had done him earlier. His gaze made me squeeze my thighs together again. I wondered if he knew that he was making me horny as hell just by looking at me.

The DJ changed the music to a Techno beat and the club suddenly seemed to get really loud. I frowned to show my dissatisfaction. If it weren't for me sitting with Jaylin at the moment, I would have gotten up and left. Pronto.

As if he could read my mind, or my face for that matter, Jaylin reached out his hand and yelled loud enough for me to hear. "Would you like to leave?"

Without giving it a second thought, I grabbed his hand and left the club with him.

"Where are we going?" I asked.

"Up to my room. It's quieter. " I tensed up a bit. He noticed and stopped to look at me. "Unless you prefer to stay down here and find a quieter place to talk. I was enjoying your company, so I figured we could continue our conversation in my room."

I pondered on whether or not going to his room was something I should do. Under normal circumstances, I wouldn't be going anywhere with him, but I felt like I knew him. I also wanted to know more about him. Pertaining to the wetness still trickling between my thighs, I wanted him to get to know me too. The inside of me.

Giving his hand a squeeze, I smiled and nodded to inform him to take the lead. That was when he asked me if I was ready for whatever would happen. I wasn't sure, but as I stood there with him, I noticed lust-filled eyes from several women who couldn't keep their eyes off of him. Their lips were pursed and they kept rolling their eyes at me. Seeing the envy in their eyes brought a surge of confidence in me. I shocked myself when I let go of his hand and turned to face him. I reached up to wrap my arms around his neck, and then I planted a soft, wet kiss on his lips. Surprisingly, he seemed flattered. My kiss had answered his question, so he grabbed my hand and continued to lead the way.

"Bitch," I heard one of the women whisper. "I bet she . . ."

I just kept it moving to Jaylin's suite in the Fontainebleau Hotel. It was amazing. Though I wasn't surprised he had a suite, seeing how he appeared made of money, I was in pure amazement at how beautiful it looked. From the large plasma TV's, to the elegance of the furniture and its layout, I was blown away. While standing near the entrance of the room, I gazed at the balcony where I could see the Atlantic Ocean.

"Would you like something to drink?" Jaylin's voice snapped me out of my thoughts. He stood in the kitchen area waiting on my response.

"Water. Water will be fine. Thank you." I walked over to the double doors that led to the balcony and looked at the amazing scenery. Jaylin grabbed a bottled water from the fridge and walked over to me.

"Beautiful, isn't it? Very relaxing." He gave the water to me.

"Yes, it really is. Very serene."

He opened the balcony doors and escorted me out. We walked past the crystal blue pool and the Jacuzzi. I stood in pure amazement, and I could see Jaylin's eyes studying me.

"You're a very beautiful woman," he complimented.

I blushed and replied to his comment. "Thank you. You're not too bad yourself."

He smiled, and all I could think of was how badly I wanted to kiss him again. He continued to study me as if I were this beautiful, exotic creature. His eyes made me feel exposed, but this time, I didn't shy away from them. I turned to face him.

"You know, your life is very intriguing," I said. "You're a different kind of man, and I must say that I've never met anyone like you before."

"Really? How is it that I'm so intriguing and different?"

I pondered on a way to tell him about what I thought of him, without being rude or judgmental. "There are so many sides to you. There is ladies' man Jaylin, husband Jaylin, father Jaylin, family man Jaylin, etcetera, etcetera. You're a very in depth person. Every time I think I have you figured out, I'm always hit with another revelation about you. When I first started reading your story, you were the most eligible bachelor in St. Louis. You also had a "girlfriend," so naturally, all I could think was . . . dirty dog."

He was tuned in and nodded as if he agreed. I continued. "You have sex with all of these women and treat them as if their disposable—As if they mean nothing to you."

"Your thoughts are interesting. Is that how you look at it?"

"Yes. And you don't?"

"Not entirely."

"Care to elaborate?"

He didn't hesitate. "There is no secret that I used to fuck a lot of women, and by the way I conduct myself, people assume that I treat women wrong. The truth is, most of the time, I give women what they want, with the exception of my heart. For some, that's good enough. For others, maybe not."

With confusion in my voice I had to ask, "Other than your heart, what else do you think the majority of them want?"

A slight smile graced his face. He leaned in close to me, almost touching my lips with his. "A mind-blowing orgasm will satisfy most."

My love nest started to contract, as if it was begging him to fuck me. I was more than ready for one of those mind-blowing orgasms, but I continued to question him.

"What makes you think that's all they want from you?"

"What really matters is what I want, and what I'm willing to give. I haven't gotten any complaints, so I assume that the majority of women I've been with are more than satisfied. Financially, as well as physically."

Shaking my head from side to side, I couldn't help but appreciate the honesty of this man. His confidence was such a turn on, and I loved how open he was with me. I was speechless, as I listened to him break it all down for me.

"Listen, baby. Pertaining to what you may think about me or how you feel about my actions, the truth is, I try my best to be honest with the women I deal with. I don't make promises I can't keep, and I'm only allowed to do what others permit. Sexually, my dick wasn't created for one woman to have. What I guarantee is fun, no boredom whatsoever, and orgasms that will never be forgotten. Dirty dog or not, take it or leave it. If they take it, then more pleasure for them. If they leave it, which most won't," he shrugged his shoulders, "oh well. Either way, I'm good."

I laughed at his blatant comment. "You are really a trip. You know that?"

"I've heard it all before."

He smiled at me then winked. I had to give the man his props—he was right. No matter what I ever thought about Jaylin, I could never say he wasn't downright blunt and honest. Well, somewhat honest, since I remembered a couple of times when he'd told lies. I called him out on it.

"I know you've heard it all before, but why did you get married and cheat on your wife? You made a promise to stay faithful to her, didn't you? What happened to that?"

He started to stroke his goatee, as if he were thinking about something.

I continued. "I'm not judging you, trust me, I'm not. I love how intriguing you are. It's crazy because—" I paused, instead of continuing my comment.

He shook his head in disapproval. "Continue. You've had a lot to say thus far, so don't stop now. Besides, I enjoy hearing about myself."

I took a deep breath, hoping that I didn't cross the line. "Well, what I was going to say was . . . I read the books and chastised you and all the women you screwed. To me, they were so stupid to continue dealing with you. But it's crazy because I also wanted to experience what it felt like to be with you. I don't know why, but—"

"I know why. Because you did judge us and you refused to look at the big picture. Those books didn't have anything to do with anyone being stupid. They were about love, commitment, challenges and real relationship struggles that many people related to. It's easy for people to attack me, based on my actions. But the bottom line is, deep down, I am a decent man. You recognize that. That's why you're curious and can't resist. If I'm being honest with you, you need to be honest with me."

The realness he was spilling and the intensity of his steel-gray eyes caused me to cream on myself. It felt like he was putting me in this trance, especially when his voice deepened. "Now, if an experience is what you want, all you have to do is ask. Is it?"

Without waiting for a response, he took a step toward me. We were now face to face. My breasts were pressed against his chest, and the feel of him made my nipples harden. He hadn't answered my earlier questions about his wife, but I was too horny to care.

"I repeat," he said. "Do you want to experience this?"

Right then, I felt his muscle swell against me. Nothing but pure sex dripped with every word that came from his mouth. The fire in his eyes was making me weak in the knees. What I should have said was, "Answer my questions and I'll answer yours." Instead, I responded, "Yes."

With that one word, his lips met with mine. His tongue invaded my mouth, causing me to moan in pleasure. We were going at it hot and heavy. That's when I felt his hand ease over my ass and lightly squeeze it. He then reached around to the front of my dress. I felt him spread my shaven pussy lips with his fingers. His eyes grew wide. "Mmm, no panties."

Using his pointer and middle fingers, he rubbed my swollen clit in slow circles. The pleasure radiating through my body made me break the kiss and moan loudly. His fingers moved slowly, but the orgasm in me was building fast. While putting more pressure on my clit, he leaned close to my ear and groaned, "You see why all that other shit we talked about doesn't matter? This wet pussy is telling me exactly what you want. But if you want to speak for yourself, please do."

I definitely couldn't deny how well *it* was speaking to him, even if I tried to. But for the moment, I remained silent. He sped up the circles, pushing me closer to the edge of orgasmic insanity.

"Tell me!" he shouted. "Tell Jay Baby what you really want."

His words sent me overboard and into the most intense climax I'd ever had. "Mmm, yeeees!" I moaned loudly. Feeling my knees buckle, I held on to his shoulders. He pulled his hand from under my dress and licked his fingers. "Sweet. Just as I expected it to be."

That shit was so sexy—I wished I were my fingers. "Now, was that all you wanted?"

By looking at me, he knew damn well that was not all I wanted. But instead of telling him, I grabbed his hand so we could go back inside. I escorted him over to the couch that was in front of the balcony in the bedroom. The couch was directly in front of another huge window that viewed the ocean. As Jaylin started to sit down, I stopped him. I reached up to unbutton his shirt, and the look of his chiseled chest sent me over the edge. Damn. Damn. Damn. This man was so fine. The muscles in his chest, abs, and arms rippled. His body looked so edible, I couldn't wait to taste him.

Lightly, I kissed his chest and licked his nipples. He groaned in pleasure and it made me want to please him more. Working my way down, I planted delicate kisses against his abs, while simultaneously unzipping his pants.

When his pants fell to the ground, my breath got hitched in my throat. I don't know how those slacks contained that damn monster. It was long with the perfect amount of thickness. Had to be the most beautiful penis I'd ever laid my eyes on. Who knew a dick could be so pretty? My mouth started to salivate at the thought of tasting him. With my eyes, I motioned for him to sit down. I squatted in front of his dick that now stood leveled at my face. Starting from the base, I took a long, slow lick up his shaft as if it were a melting popsicle. "Mmm." I moaned. He tasted so good. Using my tongue, I flicked around the tip of his dick, tasting the pre-cum that had beaded on top of it. He groaned deeply. I gripped the base of his dick and slid my wet mouth down as far as it could go. Then I slowly pulled back up. Continuously, my mouth bobbed lower and lower. Relaxing my throat, I attempted to train it to take all of him. Needless to say, I failed, but was willing to try again and again. The next time around, our eyes connected. His watching me sent me into overdrive. I was determined to please him to the fullest extent I could. And according to his groans, I was doing a damn good job.

Finally, I was able to suck him deep down my throat, without choking. Then, it was really on. The more I bobbed up and down his dick, the throatier his groans got. The feeling of his dick throbbing in my throat let me know he would be cumming for me soon. I was ready to taste every drop. Before I could prepare to take him over the edge, he gripped the sides of my face and pulled my head up.

"Not yet, baby. In a minute," he said.

Damn, talk about control. I was eager to receive his juices, but instead of giving them to me, he lowered the straps to my dress. As my straps fell, he softly kissed my shoulder. He eased my dress past my breasts and took one into his mouth. I gasped and closed my eyes. His tongue repeatedly flicked at my hard nipple. He lightly bit down on it, making my pussy cream more. His touch . . . the way he massaged my breasts together and gave the other one equal attention, it drove me crazy. I squirmed around—so much that he had to hold me up in his arms.

Seconds later, my dress hit the floor and revealed my nakedness. With every part of me now uncovered, he licked his way down. He then stepped back to look at me. I could tell he was pleased by the way he wet his lips. The hunger in his eyes made me want to devour him. Slowly, he stepped back in front of me and picked me up by my waist with ease. He sat me atop the couch with my back pressed against the window and my legs spread wide. Before I knew it, he was devouring me with his mouth. His tongue licked in between my pussy lips slow, teasing my clit. When he pulled on my clit with his soft wet lips, I moaned so loud that everyone in the building had to hear me. His pussy-sucking skills were something serious. He had taken my body to so many different levels of pleasure that I couldn't control myself.

"Jaaa . . . Jaylin," I moaned then released a deep breath.

He didn't respond, so I raked my fingers through his soft curls while he continued to lick and suck me into a sexual high.

Soon, my toes curled and my hands gripped the couch. My eyes rolled back as I was cumming hard. His licks became longer and faster, draining me of every drop. I squeezed my fists, and then . . . then I squirted his mouth with my sweet juices.

Jaylin stood and licked his lips. Coming down for my orgasmic high, I said, "That wasn't fair."

He chuckled at my words then shrugged. "Maybe not fair, but damn sure tasteful."

He moved to the side of the couch and opened another set of glass doors that led to the bed. "Come," he said, gesturing with his hand for me to follow him.

I stepped off the couch and responded with a seductive smile. We moved near the bed and he hit a button on the setup iPod radio. Maxwell's "Sumthin' Sumthin' Mellosmoothe" flowed through the speakers. It was definitely fitting for what was about to go down.

Jaylin opened a drawer and dropped a few condoms on top of the nightstand. Thank goodness for that, because as fine as he was, I was not going out like that. No way. If he didn't have them, I sure did.

As we indulged in an intense kiss, he laid me back on the bed. He then covered his rock-solid dick with a condom, while I reached out to feel his muscle-packed chest. He positioned the head of his dick right at my clit, making me wetter and wetter. The teasing tactics drove me insane. I opened my legs wider and he pushed all nine-plus inches inside of me. My walls stretched, my breathing halted and I could barely move. The size of his dick, as well as his thickness, made me feel like a virgin again.

"Relax, baby. I got you." He looked into my eyes to assure me.

I slowly exhaled, and as he entered me at a gentle pace, my pussy started to get accustomed to his big dick. The pain subsided and the pleasure came full force. I was on cloud nine as I lifted my head to share my thoughts. "Mmm, Jaylin. You feel good."

He responded by speeding up the pace and delivering deeper strokes. I wrapped my legs around his back and threw my arms around his shoulders. I had to hold on for dear life. Jaylin was stroking my insides so damn well that I couldn't do anything but repeatedly moan his name and scratch his back.

He finally replied and whispered in my ear. "I hear you, baby. Loud and clear. But I need more. Tell me more."

My eyes fluttered then shot open when he dipped in even further. "Oh my GOD! Jaaaylin! What more do you want?"

I couldn't take it. The strokes, his voice, his dick, his touch . . . everything sent me toppling into the most intense, gut-bursting orgasm ever. Trying to avoid scratching him up, I gripped the covers. What I was feeling was euphoric. My mind had been blown to pieces. My eyes fluttered again then closed. A slow tear seeped from the corner of my eye, while his tongue flicked at my nipple. This was simply amazing.

"You all right?" he asked as I cracked my eyes open to look at him. He got me . . . got me real good.

"I'm fine. But now, it's my turn. I got something for you, sir." His sexing was intimidating, but I wanted to match him.

"Show me what you got," he teased.

He pulled out of me, and a flow of my juices followed. I stood and walked over to his iPod on the desk. Grabbing it, I placed my phone onto the radio. I scrolled through to find my own created playlist.

"Looking for something?" he asked while lying back with his hands placed behind his head.

"Found it."

I pressed the button to start the playlist. Jamie Foxx's "Freakin' Me" started to play softly. Jaylin appeared very pleased by the selection. I sauntered over to him, and with his dick still at full attention, I placed a new condom over it. I stood on the bed, and then removed my heels that I'd had on the entire time. I stood with one foot on each side of him and started to move to the music. With lust locked in his eyes, he watched me perform to the sound of Marsha Ambrosius voice. My shaved pussy that displayed a tiny gap was right at his face. When I turned, my perfect ass invited him to spread it open and lick between it. This time, I had him in a trance. I saw his dick flex, telling me he was ready for me to fuck him. I inched my way down and squatted over his muscle. Positioning myself over the head, I slid down while looking him directly in his eyes. We both inhaled deeply at the same time. I was so wet that my juices could be heard throughout the room.

"Damn, baby," he said in a whisper. "You're showing out for me."

Damn right I was. Like before, he filled me to absolute capacity. I wasn't going to let up, and I fucked him to the beat of the music, nice and slow. This was my chance to take control and make him feel as good as he made me moments ago. The pleasure displayed on his face was stimulating my body more. Something about watching him unravel under me turned me on. His groans and my moans filled the room as I slow fucked him. My orgasm was building, but I couldn't let up until he was finished. Thankfully, I felt his dick pulsating inside of me and I knew I would soon get what I wanted.

"Come for me, Jay Baby. Pleeeeease," I groaned while his hands gripped my ass and massaged it.

"Keep that pussy moving like this and I damn sure will come."

His words encouraged me. Steadying my breath, I sped up and continued to work him. I was poppin' my pussy as if my name really was Diamond from *The Players Club*. And after a lengthy, satisfying ride, we both came together. I collapsed on top of him then rolled over to his side. Jaylin kissed my forehead, and then he got up to dispose of the two condoms we had just used. I looked at his sexy body in amazement, before closing my eyes and smiling.

"What are you smiling for?" he asked. I opened my eyes to see Jaylin looking over at me, smiling too. "I guess you're over there patting yourself on the back, huh?" He spoke with humor in his voice. I shrugged again. "Okay. You deserve that one. You showed me something with that good pussy of yours, but just so you know, the night isn't over yet. Far from it."

I sensed a little challenge in his voice. Even more so, the look in his eyes showed me how serious he was. He was about to put a hurting on my body. I had two choices: I could either wave the white flag now or we could fuck it out all night. Looking him square in his eyes, I welcomed his challenge and spilled the words, "Show me what you got." Needless to say, he did just that. On the balcony, in the Jacuzzi, in the shower . . . he made sure to show me on every surface that he could possibly find in his suite, exactly what he was working with.

The next morning, I woke up in Jaylin's bed. The feeling that ripped through me when I sat up had Jaylin Rogers all over it. Sore was not the word for it. I heard a faint buzz, realizing that it was my phone. I jumped up to grab it from beside the iPod radio. I answered to Marisha yelling in my ear. "Dhi'Mon, where are you! I've been calling you for over an hour!"

"I just woke up. What's wrong? You okay?" Concern was clearly in my voice.

"I'm good, but I hope you have the extra money to pay for this room. Have you seen what time it is?" I looked down at my phone to see that it was 1:43 PM.

"Shit! I'm coming!" I hung up the phone and started grabbing my clothes.

Jaylin sauntered in the bedroom with Nike basketball shorts on and the new Nike Air Max shoes on his feet. I figured he'd just come back from the fitness center. He looked at the expression on my face and asked if everything was okay.

"Yes, I mean, no. Ugh. Marisha just called and told me we're late for check out. I have to go now."

"Well, give me a second. I'll throw on a shirt and some pants and get a car to take you to your hotel."

I watched as he got naked again and quickly changed. Watching him come out of those clothes made me want to say, "Fuck it. We're already late, so do you mind if we fuck again?" But I couldn't do Marisha like that. Instead, I just put on my heels and tried my best not to jump his bones. He grabbed his wallet and we headed out the door.

Jaylin offered to get a car to take me to my hotel, but I told him that wasn't necessary because we were so close. We headed toward my hotel on foot, since it was only five minutes away and it wasn't as hot outside. I knew Marisha had to be at the hotel pissed off, especially when I made an emphasis on her being back before check out.

"I can't believe I slept so hard and didn't even hear my phone," I said underneath my breath. I looked over at Jaylin. Obviously, he'd heard me and was trying to stop himself from laughing. "What's so funny?

"All I can say, baby, is that you deserved that sleep. Even though you couldn't shut me down last night, you put up one hell of a fight." He patted my ass, and then pinched it. "Good try, though."

I couldn't help but laugh at his comment. As much as I hated to admit it, he was right. No matter what I threw at him, Jaylin fired back and worked me twice as hard. I now understood why so many women were hooked. He was the full package.

As we got closer to the hotel, I decided to follow up on our previous conversation and ask him why he couldn't keep his promise to his wife. He raked his fingers through his hair and softly touched his goatee. I thought he was about to dodge my question again, but instead he answered.

"To be honest, I wasn't trying to avoid the question last night. I thought that after our little sexual escapade, you would have your answer. It's simple, and it goes a little something like this. As long as beautiful women like you continue to throw good pussy at me, there is a possibility that I'm going to reach out and catch it. I put forth every effort to do right by Nokea, but at the time, my desires for another woman prevented me from being the husband she needed me to be. I refuse to put on a front and pretend to be someone that I'm not, so it's best that I stay uncommitted to anyone. She's good with that, and facing the truth has never hurt anyone. Because we were willing to do so, our relationship has been better than it has ever been before. That's what happens when you truly get to know and understand the one you're with, or the one you claim to love."

I couldn't argue with that. I nodded and agreed. "That is a 100% fair answer. Thank you for sharing that."

We finally got to my hotel, but before I could walk in, Jaylin stopped me. "Now, Miss Dhi'Mon, I have a question for you."

"What do you possibly have to ask me?" I asked with my brows raised.

He inched closer to me with seduction on display. "Was that all you wanted? Did I deliver on my promise to you?"

He was so lucky that we were on this sidewalk. I felt his dick press into me. Raising my hand to his chest, I pushed him back some. "Don't make me give these people out here a show. You know what you're doing."

We both saw two women standing close by, watching our entire interaction. We started laughing when they walked off whispering to each other.

"To answer your question, yes, you did deliver on your promise. That was all I wanted and then some."

That was an understatement. I'd gotten an overflow of what I had been fantasizing about for years, but I wasn't going to give him the complete satisfaction of knowing all of that. Without saying another word, we walked inside of the hotel together. Marisha was sitting in one of the lobby chairs, clearly irritated. Her irritation heightened when she saw me walk in with Jaylin.

She threw her hands up in the air and sighed. "Okay, that explains it. You were with AA over here."

Jaylin laughed, but she scowled at him.

"Girl, I'm so sorry," I said. "I'll pay the extra charge they give us. I'm sure we can work something out." I tried to calm her down. Jaylin asked us to excuse him because he needed to step away to make a call. Once he was out of earshot, I turned to Marisha, "What the hell is AA?"

She used her fingers to emphasize her words. "AA. ARROGANT. ASS."

I couldn't help but laugh at her. That's when I felt a hand on my lower back. I quickly turned to see Jaylin.

"Listen, I have to head back to my hotel room. There are a few things that I need to get done before I check out of here."

Disappointed, but content with the fact I had spent hours with him, I hugged him tight and pecked him on the lips. Before he walked off, we exchanged numbers. He then told me to have a safe flight. I assured him that I would text him when I got off the plane. One last kiss on my lips and he was gone.

"I don't like him," Marisha said as we walked up to the check-out desk. I had to use the restroom so I gave Marisha my card and key, and then walked off to the ladies room. While washing my hands, I couldn't help but reminisce about my late night and early morning with Jaylin Rogers. Although we didn't get a chance to talk a lot, I felt like I knew Jaylin on a deeper level. It made me regret passing judgment on his life. He was a good man with a good heart. People just mistook him as an asshole, when actually, he was just a man who knew what he wanted and he was honest about it. Can't be mad at that, and kudos to him because so many men were confused and downright liars.

I left the bathroom and headed to the exit where Marisha was standing. "Thanks for grabbing my bag by the way. You call a cab?" I asked her while taking my bag from her hand.

"Yup. Sure did," she answered. "Your card is in the bag. I didn't need it anyways."

I hadn't realized the wide grin on her face. "See, I told you they wouldn't trip about us being late."

"Girl, bye. They charged us for an extra day." She waved her hand back at the desk.

"What? What do you mean you didn't need the card? You paid for it?" A puzzled expression was on my face.

Marisha shook her head. "Nope. It was already paid for. Paid for in full by Mr. Rogers."

My face split into a stupid Kool-Aid smile. "Quit lying."

She shrugged and laughed. "I'm not lying. I knew there was something that I liked about his ass, but I just couldn't figure it out. Guess he wasn't so bad after all."

I shook my head. "So, I guess he isn't AA anymore?"

"Oh, no. I didn't say all of that. His ass is still arrogant. But he's cool and fine as fuck too." She nudged me and we started laughing again.

The cab we called pulled in front of the hotel. We walked on the sidewalk, carrying several bags in our hands. The driver helped us put our things in the trunk and we climbed into the backseat.

"So, what exactly did you two do last night?" Marisha questioned.

I knew she had been waiting for me to tell her what happened. I smiled at the thought of last night's festivities. Modestly I told her, "Not much. I showed him some things . . . he showed me some things. Just a night of show me what you got."

I didn't say much else, but the day I met Jaylin Rogers would be etched in my mind forever. Sex with him was so intense and mind-blowing! The more I gave to him, the more I received. He pleased my body in ways I could have never fantasized myself. It was tantalizing to say the least. Years of reading about him and trying to understand him, I thought I had him down pat. Little did I know, I knew just the bare minimum. He may not have realized it, but he gave me a lot in just those few moments of conversation we'd had. For a moment, he let me into his world, instead of shutting me down. He was honest to a fault and made no apologies for it. Others would take him as rude. But he was truly just real. I can appreciate that in anyone. His honesty was what really got me. The amazing sex just sealed the deal.

OUR LITTLE SECRET

Giana Monroe

They say lightning never strikes twice, but in my case, that phrase couldn't have been further from the truth. My Friday started out just like any other Friday, with me having the day off. I was still working with my best friend, Dr. Lamar Turner, at Turner Sports Medicine and Physical Therapy. It had been about four years, and I had finally worked my way up to having Fridays, and most weekends, off.

I hadn't planned to do much of anything, but the clinic closed early on Fridays, and Lamar wanted to get together for lunch. We decided to go to one of our favorite restaurants, Dame's Chicken & Waffles, located on West Main Street in downtown Durham, North Carolina. From the first time I visited the restaurant, at Lamar's request, I fell in love with the comfortable, yet classy, atmosphere. The building boasted beautiful white pillars that extended from floor to ceiling, while the walls were tastefully decorated with paintings of jazz greats, such as Dizzy Gillespie, Billie Holiday, Cab Calloway, Thelonious Monk, and Miles Davis. Smooth jazz played throughout the restaurant.

The food was outstanding. The main dish was, of course, chicken and waffles, served with homemade butter in varieties such as maple-pecan, peach-apricot, and vanilla-almond; but they also served seafood, salads, collard greens, mac & cheese, and tasty desserts, such as red velvet cupcakes. And the drinks . . . there was nothing like a plate of chicken and waffles served with a chilled 'pink love' strawberry mimosa.

All types of people, black, white, young, old, the wealthy, and not-so-wealthy, patronized the establishment. Lamar was a huge supporter because it was owned by several of his college buddies and fellow Omega Psi Phi fraternity brothers.

Lamar and I planned to meet around 2:00 PM, because it was after the primetime lunch rush, and before the evening dinner crowd. I reached the downtown area a few minutes before two, parked my 2014 iridescent silver blue pearl Hyundai Sonata in the small municipal parking lot, and walked the short distance to Dame's. As I entered the restaurant, I saw Lamar sitting at our usual table closest to the window. I also saw someone else, a man whom I thought I would never see again, sitting with Lamar . . . one Jaylin Jerome Rogers.

Jaylin and I met some three years and seven months ago when Lamar invited him up for North Carolina Central University's Homecoming football game. Lamar and Jaylin were old friends, and since, according to Lamar, Jaylin was the consummate host when he visited him in Miami, Lamar wanted to return the favor. As it turned out, on Jaylin's last night in town, Lamar had to work, and I was the one who ended up entertaining Jaylin. I guess I should say we ended up entertaining each other . . . with a night of hot, steamy, passionate sex that carried over into the next morning and afternoon. It was the best, and only, one-night stand I ever had.

Watching the two men, my mind quickly reflected on the fact that I never told Lamar what happened between Jaylin and me. Lamar was my best friend, and we talked about more or less of everything, but I just didn't feel right discussing my encounter with *his* friend, especially since Jaylin was known to be a player. From time to time, he would question me, asking, "Giana, what really happened between you and Jaylin?"

"Like I told you a million times before, nothing happened," I'd say. "We went out, had a few drinks, talked, danced, and basically had a great time. Then I went home. That was it."

"Yeah, that's more or less what he said," Lamar would reply, with an all-too-familiar skeptical look. "I might actually believe you two if I didn't know Jaylin so well, but I'll leave it alone. One day either you or Jaylin will slip up, and the truth will come out." So far, it hadn't come out, and I was hoping to keep it that way.

Jaylin was still as handsome as ever with his curly back hair, moustache and goatee that were flawlessly trimmed, and those hypnotic gray eyes. And by the way his Brooks Brothers Regent Fix Saxxon Wool Bead Stripe 1818 suit fit, I could tell he still worked out frequently. When I last saw Jaylin, he had the body of a chiseled Zulu warrior, except his complexion was quite a few shades lighter, like that of light maple dipped in honey.

"Damn," he said. "Dr. Monroe. Long time no see." He got up from his seat and leaned down to kiss me on the cheek. "Lookin' good, baby," he whispered in my ear. I wasn't much into makeup, and today was no exception, but I was still looking cute. My locks were curled in ringlets and hung down to my shoulders. I was glad I decided to wear my tiny bling light colored denim jeans, light blue off-the-shoulder top, and flats, instead of my usual Nike gear and high-top sneakers. The outfit accentuated my petite, yet shapely frame.

I returned his kiss on the cheek. "You're looking pretty good yourself, Jaylin. I am happy to see you, but I'm surprised to see you here."

As I took my seat at the table, Lamar chimed in. "Jaylin's in town on business. He's looking to invest in the 21c Museum Hotel project down the block." The 21c Museum Hotel project was going to be huge. Developers planned to convert the old 17-story Hill Bank Building into a 125-room boutique hotel, with a restaurant/bar, and a museum that would show contemporary art. The model was to be based off the other 21c hotel museums in Louisville, Kentucky; Cincinnati, Ohio; and Bentonville, Arkansas. Not only would the project open up more jobs in Durham, it would also attract more locals and tourists to the area. I could see why Jaylin wanted to be a part of such a major undertaking. It would add very nicely to his already extensive portfolio.

We were about to continue our conversation when our waiter, Marcus, came over. "Hey everybody. What can I get for you today?" Once pleasantries were exchanged, we all placed our food orders. I chose Dame's Daily Deal with fried chicken legs, a classic waffle, and maple-pecan butter, while the guys both selected the blacken salmon with a side salad. For our drinks, Jaylin asked for a glass of Remy, his usual drink of choice. Lamar picked a Triangle White Ale for himself, and for me, a strawberry mimosa.

Once our orders were in, Jaylin continued where Lamar left off. "I just came from a big meeting with some other investors, and I hit up Lamar. I wanted to see if he was interested in investing too. He told me you two were meeting for lunch, so I figured I'd join you. I hope you don't mind," he said, flashing me a dazzling smile in that flirtatious way of his.

"Now, Jaylin, why in the world would I mind?" I asked, giving him my best flirtatious smile in return.

"Oh boy, here we go again." Lamar sighed.

"Man, come on. You know the good doc and I are cool like that. This is just how we do," Jaylin remarked. "So, Giana, what have you been up to?"

I usually don't mind when people ask that question, but for some reason it bothered me when Jaylin did it. "Nothing much. Work mostly. And you?"

And then I saw it; that look that said Jaylin was about to get all up in my business. The last time that happened, he found out way too much about my personal life, and he used it against me. That wasn't going to happen this time, or so I hoped. "What, no boyfriend?"

Yep, I called that one. "No, Jaylin, I'm currently single."

"And why is that?"

"Just busy I guess." I felt the heat rising in my cheeks.

Lamar snickered. "She's not that busy. She's just avoiding men."

I shot Lamar a steely glance. "Lamar . . ."

"What? I thought you and Jaylin were cool."

"We are, but—"

He quickly cut me off. "But what? We're all friends, right? So what's the harm in telling one friend why another friend is scared to date, hmmmm?"

I found Lamar's ribbing at my expense less than amusing. I sucked my teeth, and gave him a serious side eye. "Whatever, Lamar."

Jaylin noticed how irritated I was and interjected. "Lamar cut her some slack. If she doesn't want to talk about it, she doesn't have to." In that moment, I really appreciated Jaylin for having my back. "Besides, it can't be any worse than that damn thirty-second lover she dated for five long years. That mutha fucka was just lame." And just that quickly, the moment was gone. He and Lamar laughed so loudly people turned to look.

"I hate you two so much right now, really I do," I snarled, crossing my arms in front of me.

Lamar got up and hugged me, despite the fact that I sat there stiff as a board. "Aww come on now, G, you know we're just messing with you."

"Lamar, you don't see me bringing up your last relationship fiasco. You remember the crazy chick who was trying to have your baby by putting holes in her diaphragm?"

He quickly released me from his grip. "Ouch! See, why you have to go there, Giana?"

"Doesn't feel so good when you're in the hot seat, does it, Lamar?" I didn't give him time to respond. Instead, I turned to Jaylin. "Mr. Rogers, if you must know, I'm single because my last boyfriend ended up being a big time stalker."

Jaylin raised an eyebrow. "Stalker? What kind of stalker?"

"Phone stalker, cyber stalker, in-person stalker, take your pick."

"Damn, what did you do to make him stalk you?"

I stared at Jaylin for a few long seconds before responding. "I didn't do anything to *make* him stalk me. Long story short, he couldn't deal with me and Lamar being friends, even though I never gave him a reason to think we were anything but. One time, he even showed up at the job and started some mess with Lamar."

Jaylin looked at Lamar. "And you didn't beat that son-of-a-bitch's ass?"

"Nah, man, as much as I would have liked to, I didn't. Not a good look for the practice. Besides, I don't have Jaylin Jerome Roger's money to hire a high-powered lawyer to get me off from an assault charge," Lamar said, shaking his head. "Plus, this one here begged me not to," he said, thumbing in my direction.

Jaylin scowled. "Fuck that. I would have beaten the shit out of that mutha fucka, and then I would have dared his ass to call the cops. I'm just sayin'."

I continued with my story. "Anyway, because he showed out, that was the last straw. I kicked his sorry behind to the curb. Needless to say, he was pissed. That's when the blocked phone calls started. Then I started getting emails from a strange email address. I traced all of them back to my nutty ex. That's when I got the order of protection."

"Hell, those things don't work. It's just a piece a paper," Jaylin noted as our food arrived.

"You ain't lyin' bro," Lamar added. "That fool started following her. We called the cops on him a few times, but since he left before they got there, they couldn't do much."

Jaylin took a sip of his Remy. "I'm telling you, one good ass whoopin' would have shut ole boy down."

"Or it could have made him act out even more," I retorted.

"The way I would have kicked his happy ass, he wouldn't have been in any condition to retaliate." He finished off his first glass and signaled for Marcus to bring him another.

I ran my palms down the front of my face, placing my chin on my thumbs. "Well, since I couldn't beat him up, I got him locked up instead. It won't be for much longer, but, at least, it's something."

"You better hope he doesn't start again, once he's out." Jaylin stopped eating just long enough to comment.

"Are you speaking from experience, Jaylin?" I inquired.

"Hell, yeah, I am. Some of you women are insane." He and Lamar gave each other a pound.

"What did *you* do to make a woman stalk you?" I asked with a smile on my face.

"Giana, what makes you think I did *anything* to get stalked?" He had a mischievous glint in his eyes. I didn't respond. Instead, I tilted my head to the side and gave him a look that said, 'Come on, Jaylin, really?' That caused him to smile and reply, "All I'll say is that once a woman gets a taste of Jay Baby, she's gonna want more. If she can't get it, she may lose her mind." He sat back smugly.

"I ain't mad atcha, bro, I ain't mad," Lamar said admiringly.

I had another eye roll moment. "If you say so." I can admit to myself that the sex with Jaylin was phenomenal, but I definitely had not lost *my* mind. Must be something in the Miami air, or the water, that made women go all *Snapped* over Jaylin Jerome Rogers.

Just as Jaylin was about to say something, Lamar's phone rang. It was the office. He rose from the table. "Excuse me you two. I have to take this. Talk amongst yourselves until I get back," he said with a grin.

I waited until he stepped outside before turning my attention to Jaylin. "How have you been?"

"I'm good, baby, but I'm always good." He winked as he said that.

"Did you ever get back together with that special lady of yours?" Now it was my turn to be nosy.

"No, not yet. I'm still giving her some space. In the meantime, I'm just doin' me right now." He took a sip of his second glass of Remy. "Although I'd rather do you."

I laughed; it was more out of nervousness than anything. For some reason, Jaylin had that effect on me. Of course, I'd never let him know that. "Been there, done that. I'm good," I remarked, trying to sound nonchalant.

"But we had such a good time, didn't we?"

I couldn't argue with that. Being with Jaylin was one of the best nights of my life, a night I would never forget, but there was more to life than great sex, for me anyway. "Yes, Jaylin, it was amazingly incredible, but I'm just not up for another casual fling." I broke my own rules by not only having casual sex, but a one-night stand on top of it. While I didn't regret it, I wasn't sure how I felt about going there again.

Jaylin moved a bit closer to me. I looked out the window to make sure Lamar wasn't watching us. "Why not, Giana? Oh wait, I know. You're still looking for Mr. Right. Well, baby, he ain't here, I am. So until your Mr. Right comes along, why not go for Mr. Right Now? At least you know with me what you see is what you get." I had to give it to Jaylin. While I hated his psychobabble assessment of me, he was right. Mr. Rogers was one of *the* rudest, most arrogant, and at times extremely irritating and overwhelmingly infuriating men to ever cross my path. At the same time, he was also very insightful, incredibly honest, and definitely one of the realest people I had ever met. "How long has it been, Giana?"

"Well, it's May, so the last time we saw each other was three years and seven months ago, give or take."

Jaylin gave me a slick smile. "Funny how you remember almost exactly how long it's been since we'd last seen each other, but that's not what I was asking. I mean, how long has it been since you got some?"

I sat there, deciding whether or not to answer him. I tried to deflect instead. "I would have to say much longer than it's been for you," I remarked, trying not to show how uncomfortable I was, knowing where the conversation was headed.

"Sweetheart, unlike you, you know Jay Baby never denies himself of anything I want," he replied, that familiar smug look on his face. "But that does not answer my question." Leaning in even closer, he asked slowly, "How . . . long . . . has . . . it . . . been?"

When Jaylin wanted to know something, he was like a pit bull with a bone in its teeth; he just wasn't going to let it go. Sighing, I gave him an answer, "One year, three months and counting."

Jaylin almost spit out his Remy. "You serious?"

I pursed my lips and looked at him. "Would I lie about that? Especially to you?"

He gave me a long, probing glance, as if trying to see if I was messing with him. "Damn. Well, I already know you're not a fan of casual sex, except with me of course."

I sat back in my chair and raised an eyebrow. "I just love how you have the uncanny ability to turn a conversation into something about you."

"It's a gift, baby." He winked at me again. "Give me your phone."

"Why?"

Instead of answering me, he simply held out his hand. I hesitated, but in the end surrendered my phone to him. I watched as Jaylin tapped the Richnote app on the screen and typed something. I tried to look over his shoulder, but he shifted his position in his chair so I couldn't see. When he finished, he gave me my phone and said, "Don't look at it until you're in your car." There was a gleam in Jaylin's eyes that said he was up to no good, and that I might be in trouble before the day was over.

Lamar finally finished his phone call. He instantly observed the intense vibe between Jaylin and I. "Am I interrupting something?"

Turning to look at him, I replied, "Not at all. Jaylin and I were just catching up."

Lamar looked first at me, then at Jaylin. I knew Lamar well enough to know he was suspicious, but he knew me well enough not to push the issue, especially in front of Jaylin. "Okay, well, I gotta get going. I need to find coverage for tomorrow afternoon. One of the high schools called last minute for an extra doc to be on site, and if I don't find someone, I might get stuck covering myself. Unless, Gia—"

I quickly raised my hand, stopping him mid-sentence. "No way, Lamar. This is my weekend off, and I am going to enjoy it."

"And do what?"

"It doesn't matter. It's my weekend OFF." I laughed.

He laughed with me. "Fine, but if I'm stuck covering, I'm blaming you. Jaylin, some of my frat brothers and I are supposed to have a business meeting tomorrow then head to the sports bar. I don't want to miss that."

"I'm sure you'll find someone to fill in, Lamar." I looked at my watch then stood from my chair. "I have to get home too."

"To do what?" he asked quizzically.

"The same thing I do most nights; work out, shower, and watch TV. You know me. I'm predictable."

Lamar shook his head. "Yep, you can set your watch by you. Well, you go on, and I'll call you later. Jay, hold up for a second while I settle up the bill." Lamar walked over to the bar to pay our tab.

Jaylin stood and looked at me. The way he was eyeing me was unnerving. "It was good seeing you again, Jaylin. Maybe I'll see you again in another three years," I teased.

"Maybe sooner, if you decide to do something unpredictable." He leaned down and gave me a tight hug. "Don't forget to check your phone."

I returned his hug. Once we broke contact, I nodded. I waved to Lamar and headed for the parking lot. Once I was in my car, I pulled out my phone and looked at Jaylin's note. It read:

Washington Duke Inn & Golf Club
Presidential Suite
9:00 PM sharp
Don't disappointment me Giana
All love,
Jaylin

I stared at the message for a few minutes before placing my phone back in the holster. Clearly that wasn't an invitation nor was it a request, it was a demand. Yes sir, when Jaylin Jerome Rogers wanted something, or someone, he had no problem making his demands known. And he was used to getting what he wanted. I had to admire that type of boldness. However, that did not mean he was going to get his way this time around. Jaylin Jerome Rogers wasn't the boss of me.

I spent the thirty-minute drive home thinking about Jaylin's message, and what he said about Mr. Right Now. It would be so easy to give in to him again. But why should I? What was I getting out of it, other than another night of mind-blowing, phenomenal sex and some pretty good conversation? When it was all said and done, I'd probably be left feeling somewhat empty inside. Seeing him again brought back good memories of the short time we spent together, and sure I was still attracted to him, but it also reminded me that I wanted more. Not necessarily from Jaylin, because he obviously wasn't the settle down, relationship type of man. As Jaylin so aptly coined him, Mr. Right. I just had no clue who that was or where to find him.

As I pulled into the garage of my three-story Chapel Hill condo, I tried to put everything out of my mind. After I got out of my car, I disarmed and reset my house alarm, took off my shoes, and ran up to my bedroom to change. I threw off my street clothes, tossing them in the hamper in my walk-in closet. I grabbed a pair of light blue and black workout shorts, and a matching sports bra, off of the shelf with my exercise clothes, and quickly got dressed. I ran back downstairs, stopping in the kitchen to grab a bottle of water from the refrigerator then headed for my home gym, which was located in the basement.

The plan was to work up a really good sweat in order to get rid of all the pent up sexual tension I was feeling. I typically did, at least, an hour of cardio, which was usually consisted of two different videos. I wanted to make myself really tired, because if I was exhausted enough, I wouldn't even think about leaving the house to meet up with Jaylin. I selected a high intensity dance video, and a cardio kickboxing video. I turned on my DVD player and 50 inch television, popped in the first video, and got to work, hoping to distract myself. I finished both videos, but try as I might, I couldn't keep my mind off of today. In fact, I was even more hyped, and my thoughts were racing non-stop. As I turned off the TV and DVD player, I wished I could turn off my thoughts the same way, and not think about Jaylin, and what could possibly happen tonight if I allowed it.

Maybe my long hiatus from having sex was finally getting the better of me, or maybe seeing Jaylin again stirred up something in me that I thought was dead and buried. Whatever the reason, the more I mulled over it, the more I realized that I wanted to be with him again, even if it was only for one night.

I checked the time before hopping in the shower. It was only 7:45 PM; plenty of time to prepare myself for what was, most likely, going to be a very long night. Once I showered and dried off, I applied some homemade shea and cocoa body butter, and some honey nut scented oil to my skin. I wasn't sure what I wanted to wear, then I thought about it; whatever I wore, most likely, wasn't going to stay on too long anyway. Jaylin wanted unpredictable, he was going to get it. And if I was going to do this, I was going to do it big. I took out my white Victoria's Secret Very Sexy Georgette halter babydoll and matching panties from the drawer and placed them on the bed. I matched the outfit with a pair of white 1 ½" heel rhinestone sandals.

By the time I donned the ensemble and packed an overnight bag, it was 8:25 PM, enough time to get to Jaylin's hotel before his 9:00 PM deadline. Checking my coat closet, I grabbed my black knee length spring coat, making sure I buttoned it all the way up, and tied the belt securely. I wanted to make a bold impression, but only to Jaylin.

I set my alarm, locked up, and got on my way. I drove most of the way on US 15-501 N, and even though it was a Friday night, traffic to Durham was still flowing pretty well. I arrived at The Washington Duke Inn & Golf Club with ten minutes to spare. I knew Jaylin only stayed at the finest hotels, and this one was no exception. The hotel was a huge 'L' shaped building situated on an expansive golf course. I parked my car and grabbed my overnight bag, anxious to see what the Presidential Suite looked like. Jaylin only laid his head in the lap of luxury, so I could only assume it was magnificent.

I wanted to avoid asking for directions, so I bypassed the front desk and headed straight to the elevator. Luckily, there was a map with suite locations on the elevator wall. The Presidential Suite was on the top floor. As I pressed the button, I felt a wave of nervous excitement overtake me. That feeling would soon be replaced by awe when Jaylin answered my knock at the door. He was standing there in all his magnificence, wearing nothing but a pair of black boxer briefs. The man's body was still a wonder to behold, sculpted to perfection. And the bulge in his shorts, well, let's just say bigger was definitely better. I couldn't help but openly ogle him from head to toe for a few seconds.

He broke me out of my daze when he asked, "Still see something you like?" Those were the same words he asked the night of our first encounter.

"But, of course." I gave him a wink.

Jaylin chuckled. I think I actually made him blush. "You're early, but not too early. I like that."

"I figured you would." I stepped inside the foyer and was immediately astounded. The Presidential Suite was massive. From the foyer, one could see the sizable dining room with a large mahogany table and six chairs. Next was the ample sitting room with a couch, two ornate chairs, and a seti. A mahogany coffee table sat in front of the couch, while matching two end tables with decorative lamps sat on either side of the couch.

"Nice, isn't it?" Jaylin asked, as I surveyed the area.

"Very. I'm impressed."

"If you like this, you should see some of the other hotels I've stayed in. Here, let me get your coat." I unbuttoned my coat and handed it to Jaylin. After he hung it up in the front closet, he said, "Turn around." I felt like I was on display, but did as he asked.

He gave me a wide smile. "Very nice, Giana. I approve this outfit."

I took off my shoes, also placing them in the closet. "So glad you approve," I replied, shaking my head. Now, if you don't mind, can you please show me to the bedroom?" I asked picking up my bag.

"Of course I don't mind. Follow me." He took me by the hand and escorted me to the bedroom. It boasted a California

King bed with a solid oak headboard, a matching dresser and chest of drawers, a 47 inch television, minibar, small refrigerator, a desk, and a lounger. On top of the minibar was a bottle of Remy, and what appeared to be a bottle of wine. After placing my bag in the bedroom closet, Jaylin poured himself a glass of Remy. He then poured a glass from the tall, dark blue wine bottle and handed it to me.

"Thank you," I said. I took a sip and realized it was Moscato D'Asti, and a very expensive one at that. I had a couple of glasses the first time Jaylin and I went out. I was surprised he actually remembered. I thought that was rather sweet of him.

"You're welcome. I wasn't sure you were going to show up." Jaylin sat down on the oversized bed.

"To be honest with you, I wasn't sure I was going to show up either," I replied, joining him. "But I decided why not go for what I wanted? And tonight, what I want is you."

Polishing off his drink, Jaylin said, "You made the right choice. But then again, I'm always the right choice." He showed off those perfect teeth of his.

I laughed too. "The truth according to Jaylin." I finished my drink and placed it on the nightstand, and then took Jaylin's empty glass and did the same. "Well, Mr. Rogers, here's my bit of truth," I responded, straddling him, and putting my arms around his neck. "Tonight is about fulfilling a need, and I anticipate leaving here a happy woman. Think you can make that happen?"

Jaylin gave a hearty laugh. "Woman, how dare you ask me that? Last I checked, you were *very* happy and satisfied the last time we were together."

"Ah true, but that was then, this is now. I'll just say let the games begin."

This time around, I made the first move and kissed him first. His lips were as soft as I remembered. I put my tongue in his mouth, tasting the Remy still on his breath. Jaylin lay back on the bed, bringing me down on top of him. His hands reached underneath my babydoll, running them up and down my smooth milk chocolate hued skin. We were still locked in a kiss, when he turned us both over. He was now on top of me and moving us both toward the center of the bed.

Jaylin's lips moved down to my neck. As he pressed his hard body against mine, I felt his rock solid member growing. He pulled my babydoll over my head, placing it to the side. His wet, warm mouth moved down even further to my breasts, causing a hiss to escape from my lips. He planted slow kisses along my body, past my belly ring, stopping at my panties. He kissed my hairless kitty through my panties. Moving them to the side, I felt his tongue move up and down my damp folds. I closed my eyes and took deep breaths, thoroughly enjoying what Jaylin was doing to me. He moved to my clitoris, sucking on it gently. His arms wrapped around my thighs, holding me in place, while his tongue fluttered like a butterfly back and forth. I was on the verge of an orgasm, the first of many that night, and Jaylin knew it. My grip tightened on the sheets as his tongue parted my lips, and my juices started to flow for what seemed like forever.

When I finally relaxed, Jaylin came up for air. "Umm umm umm. Still tasty. I can't wait to get my dick in that wet pussy."

"Why wait when it's here for the taking?" I removed my panties then began pulling down Jaylin's briefs, all the while knowing I was talking smack. I mean seriously, who was I kidding? I'd be lucky to survive with my coochie intact. I needed several icepacks and painkillers just to recover after my last bout with Jaylin. Thing is, I enjoyed our trash talk, and despite everything, I planned to give my all.

Once Jaylin removed his briefs, I got a full view of his extra-large appendage, all nine-plus inches. If penises could be considered pretty, Jaylin's would be at the top of that list. I wanted him so bad, I could taste it. He rubbed the tip between my soaking wet folds, ready to enter the Promised Land, when a thought occurred to me. I had completely forgotten to pack some condoms. Not that Jaylin would have minded, because he never liked using them anyway. Last time, he tried to argue me down about having to wear one. I won that battle, but this time I wasn't so sure. One thing I did know, he was going to be furious with me. "Jaylin?"

"Yeah?" He looked up at me.

"I know my timing kind of sucks right now, but I don't have any condoms," I said, slowly edging away from him.

Jaylin raised up, a look of annoyance on his face. "And? Come the fuck on, Giana. You know how I feel about those damn things."

"And you know I won't do anything without them." Usually, it was Jaylin's way or no way. But not this time, and not in this situation. Jaylin already knew my stance; no glove, no love. We appeared to be at an impasse, which was a shame because I was so ready for him and the nine plus. I guess Jaylin got tired of the stare down, because he eventually reached into his nightstand drawer and pulled out a box of Lifestyle Skyn Large condoms.

"Happy now?"

I gave him my widest grin. "Jaylin, you did this for me?"

Still annoyed, he replied, "HELL NO!" I just looked at him. "You made such a big damn deal the last time that I knew if I didn't have one, you weren't giving up the pussy. Hell, I did this for me." I wanted to be mad at Jaylin, but all I could do was laugh. I knew deep down, in some small way, he liked me enough to respect my wishes. He opened the box, handing me a condom. "Here," he said. "You know the deal. You want me to wear this so badly, you put it on ya damn self."

Like I was going to say no. I took his still hard erection in my hand, stroking it a few times. "Thank you, Jaylin." I slid the condom down, making sure it was secure.

Giving me a side eye, he replied, “Yeah, yeah. Let’s see if you’re still thanking me when you need that icepack.”

“Promises, promises,” I retorted.

“This ain’t no damn promise, it’s a straight up threat. That pussy is about to get pounded.” He started to lower himself on top of me. “Think you can handle it?”

“Stop talking and bring it already.” I pulled him down the rest of the way, planting a kiss on his lips, waiting for him to take out his frustrations on me. He inserted one finger inside me, I assumed to see if I was still wet. Then I felt it; the first few of his nine-plus inches, entering me slowly. As expected, I felt some pain, but not enough to make him stop. His strokes were long, slow, and deliberate. The pain gave way to exquisite pleasure. Jaylin and I had been here before, so he knew exactly what spots to hit.

Giving me all of him, he placed his lips close to my ear, whispering, “Sure you can handle all this dick?”

Instead of answering him, I wrapped my legs around his waist, matching him stroke for stroke, thrust for thrust. Jaylin raised himself up onto his knees, bringing me up with him. I felt him all the way up my lower back. If my cervix wasn’t in his way, he probably would have been hitting my liver. He stood up, walked over to a wall, and pinned me against it. He wrapped one arm around my slender waist and held my arms above my head with the other. “Damn, this is some good pussy.”

“You’re not . . . so bad yourself . . . Jaylin.” I was about to explode again. “Don’t stop . . . yes . . . right there.” My breathing heightened, as Jaylin pushed harder, bringing me to climax a second time.

Still inside me, he walked back to the bed. He positioned me in the middle of the bed with my head on the pillows. By now, I had more or less adjusted to Jaylin’s length and girth. I felt a bit more daring, so I tightened my muscles around his nine. I knew I was getting to him when I heard him mutter,

"Fuck." I kept on doing it, eliciting a few more profane words from his mouth. "You might wanna stop that," he remarked.

Not stopping I asked, "Why?"

"Because doing that can get you in trouble."

"When it comes to you, I like trouble," I replied, looking him squarely in the eyes.

"Big talk for such a little person," he teased. In one swift motion, Jaylin flipped me over, raising my backside in the air. He took me from behind, long stroking me. "Let's see how big you talk now." It felt so good, I started biting a pillow. I attempted to move back on him, but he stopped me. "I got this baby."

I never had a man take me from behind and have it feel so incredible. Each thrust was bringing me closer to reaching my peak. Just as it was about to happen, his phone rang. I turned my head and saw him looking over to the nightstand to see who it was. He reached for the phone, answering it. I don't know which was more disturbing; the fact that he answered the phone, the fact that he put it on speaker or the fact that he kept going. "Hey, Lamar, what's up?" By now it was well past eleven. Why would Lamar be calling him this late? I looked back at him, confused. He just smiled and put his finger to his lips, signaling for me to be quiet. With his free hand, he held on to my hip, preventing me from breaking free.

Seriously? With the way he was tapping my G-spot, did he really expect me to not make a sound? I buried my face in the pillow in order to quiet my moans, all the while listening to his conversation with Lamar. "Yo, Jay, sorry for calling so late. Were you busy?"

"I was in the middle of my workout." I turned around again, frowning. He shrugged, a smile still on his face.

"Okay, I'll make this quick. I found coverage for tomorrow, so I'm good to go. Also, I spoke with the guys, and they're all set for the meeting tomorrow."

"Good. Everybody can meet here in my room at one o'clock. You know how I am, so everybody better be on time, or I'll start without them. After the meeting, we can get in a round or two of golf then hit up that sports bar you were talking about."

"Sounds like a plan. I'll pass the word. And, Jay, sorry for the interruption. Later."

"Later, man." Jaylin disconnected the call and replaced his phone on the nightstand. "Sorry, baby. I promise you, no more interruptions. You, and this pussy, have my undivided attention." Grabbing both my hips, Jaylin began to drive himself into me harder and faster. His nine felt like a titanium rod. He was about to erupt and so was I. The faster he pumped, the harder I came until we both collapsed in a heap on the bed.

Good thing we finished when we did, because not five minutes later, my phone began to vibrate. I grabbed it from the nightstand, showing Jaylin the caller ID before answering. It was Lamar. "Hello?" I answered in a sleepy voice. Jaylin shook his head as he got up to go to the bathroom.

"Hey, G. I was going to invite you for some late night IHOP, but I guess you're asleep."

I hated lying to Lamar, but I was not comfortable with him knowing what I was up to, and with whom. "Yeah, that workout really wore me out." I laughed to myself at the double meaning. "But we can hang out later this weekend if you're not too busy with Jaylin."

"Works for me. Go back to sleep, and we'll talk later."

"Okay, good night." I touched the screen to end the call. I got out of bed and waited for Jaylin to finish in the bathroom. As we switched places, he looked at me and again shook his head. "What?" I asked.

"Nothing," he replied. I ignored him for the moment, taking my turn in the bathroom.

When I came back, Jaylin was relaxing on the bed with his back against the headboard, a fresh glass of Remy in hand.

He motioned for me to join him. I walked over to his side of the bed then sat in between his legs with my back leaning against him. As I turned slightly to face him, he handed me a glass of Moscato D'Asti. It hit the spot, considering how parched I was. "You okay?" Jaylin asked.

I looked into his beautiful gray eyes. "I'm fine. Sore, but otherwise fine," I laughed.

Jaylin chuckled. "I thought you could handle it."

"You were there. I did handle it," I replied. "But now I'm paying for it."

Adding more Remy to his glass, he uttered, "Well, you know we're not done yet. The night is still young and you're not leaving here anytime soon."

I held out my glass for another drink. "Trust me, Jaylin, I know. I wasn't planning on going anywhere."

"Good," he replied, refilling my glass. "So, let me ask you this, Giana; why did you lie to Lamar when he called you? Why didn't you want him to know you were with me?"

I thought about it for a moment before answering. "To be honest with you, I guess I care what he thinks about me. And for the record, you lied to him too. 'I was in the middle of my workout'," I chortled, imitating Jaylin.

Jaylin couldn't help but laugh. "You know damn well that wasn't a lie. I might have omitted some major details, but I *was* in the middle of a workout. I was sweating and everything. But if you want to go there, you owe me."

"How you figure?" I couldn't wait to hear his explanation.

"I compromised my principles by not being 100% honest. I did that for you," he said, pretending to be wounded.

I found Jaylin hilarious. He had this knack for turning a situation around and using it to his advantage. "Sure, Jaylin, you did it for me. And why would you do that?"

"You said it yourself; you care what he thinks about you. I was just protecting your good name."

Once again, Jaylin used my own words against me. This man was full of it, but I couldn't help but play along. "Fine. What are your terms?"

"I'm not sure . . . yet. But when I'm ready to collect, just be ready to pay up, no questions asked."

"Hmmmm, you get to call in a marker whenever you feel like it, and I basically have no say in the matter. Sounds like blackmail to me."

"Consider it a business arrangement with very narrow terms. Default is not an option," he responded, a self-satisfied look on his face.

I was actually intrigued and wanted to see how this would eventually play out. "Jaylin, you have got yourself a deal."

"Wise choice. Now, tell me, have you and Lamar ever . . . ?"

I cut him off mid-sentence. "Oh God no, never! Lamar is my best friend, more like a big brother. An overly protective big brother, but that is it."

"Good to know because I don't do sloppy seconds. I don't have too much respect for a woman who sleeps with a man, then let's his boy hit it. But that still begs the question as to why you care what Lamar thinks. Hell, why do you care what anyone thinks? I'll be damned if I care what anyone thinks about me."

I looked at him, raising an eyebrow. "Clearly. But to answer your question, while you may not care about how others perceive you, I do care how they see me. My reputation is everything, personally and professionally. And let's face it Jaylin; you're a bad boy in really expensive clothing. While Mitt Romney had a binder full of women, you, my friend, probably have an electronic Rolodex full of them. You've been with a lot of women, and Lamar knows that. And as much as I'm enjoying this, I don't want to be seen as just another entry in that Rolodex."

"You, Dr. Monroe, are not just another entry in my so-called electronic Rolodex. Hell, I didn't even know there was an app for that," he said, mirth in his tone. Jaylin lifted my chin, forcing me to look him in the eyes. "If you were, we wouldn't be here like this. The way I see it is this; we are friends and two consenting adults who really enjoy each other's company, and I don't just mean the sex. Whatever happens, whenever it happens, it's just between us. Cool?"

In some small way, I felt like I got to know a bit more about this man whom I still knew very little. "Cool. And, Jaylin, thank you," I said, kissing him on the cheek.

"You're welcome, baby. But there's something you should know."

I was almost afraid to ask. "What's that?"

Flashing me a sly grin, Jaylin stated, "Once the pussy's mine, it's always mine."

"Say what now?" I crossed my arms in front of me, rolling my neck.

"You heard me woman. Once mine, always mine."

It was funny how some men are of the mindset that they can keep a woman's coochie, or several women's for that matter, on lock, demanding her complete loyalty, but then go around slangin' community penis. And yet, I was amused by Jaylin's sheer audaciousness. Currently, I was very unattached, so I had no problem letting Jaylin think it was his . . . for now. "I'll keep that under advisement."

"You'd better," he said. "One more thing. I'm not sure if you've realized it, but I'm not your one-night stand anymore."

"You're right, you're not. Now you're my two-night stand," I kidded.

A devilish look in his eyes, Jaylin replied, "I don't leave until Sunday. Play your cards right and we can make it three."

"Throw in dinner tomorrow night and it's a date," I said, extending my hand for him to shake in agreement.

He gently pushed my hand away and instead kissed me on the forehead. "You got it, sweetheart."

"In that case, I say we pick up where we left off," I said, taking another condom out of the box, sheathing his rock hard nine-plus inches. "After all, once you leave, who knows when we'll see each other again?"

"Who knows indeed?" Jaylin answered. "But then again, it might be sooner than you think," he countered, turning me around to face him and slipping himself inside of me.

One could only hope. I kissed Jaylin deeply, enjoying the time, and everything else, he was giving me, even if it was only for a short while.

And there you have it. For me lightning did strike twice, and if my luck held, it might strike a third time. I may not have had my Mr. Right, but for the time being, I did have Mr. Right Now, Jaylin Jerome Rogers, a man who appears to come into my life exactly when I need him, and someone I actually consider to be a friend. Like Mr. Rogers said, whatever happens, whenever it happens, it's just between us and it would remain our little secret.

MY DADDY

Myra Walker

The day Jaylin Rogers crossed my path, I was putting groceries into the trunk of my car. Two of my bags ripped, sending several of my items rolling down the parking lot. My bread was smashed and every last one of my eggs were cracked. I was frustrated, only because I warned the bagger about putting too many items in one bag. But much of my frustrations went away, when I spotted a very sexy and clean-cut man pick up my rolling items and carry them in his arms. A white, polo cap covered his curly hair and the cap matched his shirt. He wore tan cargo shorts that showed his toned calves, and leather sandals covered his feet. I was tongue-tied by how handsome he was and could barely get out the word, "Thanks." He smiled at the shocking look on my face, and after conversing with him for about thirty minutes, he gave me his phone number. I couldn't wait to call him, and later that day, we spoke further about our careers, family and friends. He invited me to his place the following day, and being from Miami, I knew the area he mentioned was where many of the rich and famous people lived. He mentioned that he was a property investor, but when I parked in front of his house, I couldn't believe how spectacular it was. Glass windows surrounded the place, and the stone columns made the house appear fit for a king. Palm trees adorned the property and it was so bold and beautiful that it made many of the other properties in the same vicinity look ordinary. The nearby ocean was a bonus, and there was easy access to the white, sandy beach. I was floored, but even more when Jaylin opened the double doors to let me inside.

"What's up, Myra," he said with a Crest smile that made my heart melt. I didn't want to appear loony or out of my mind, but the truth is I was blown away.

"Hi, Jaylin. How are you?"

I reached out to give him a hug. Being snuggled against his chest sent me to la-la land, and since I was so short and petite, his tallness made me feel very secure in his arms.

"I'm good, baby, can't complain. Why don't you step into the living room and have a seat. I'm waiting for my nanny to return, so that you and I can have some privacy."

I stepped down into the sunken living room with all white furniture. A winding staircase made of glass and wood was to my right, and to the left was a humongous fireplace with a flat screen TV mounted above it. I was careful not to mess up anything, as I stepped on the white, plush carpet, and hopefully, I didn't sweat when I sat on the leather sectional.

"Can I get you anything?" Jaylin asked then looked at his watch.

I needed to clear my dry throat, so I asked for a glass of ice water.

Jaylin left the room, and I looked up at the tall, vaulted ceilings. Near the staircase were doors to several rooms, and standing right by a loft area was a little girl. She was very pretty and Jaylin's look was written all over her. A teddy bear was squeezed in her arms, and as she saw me looking at her, she smiled. I waved at her, but when Jaylin came back into the room with my water, I turned my head toward him.

"Thank you," I said, removing the glass from his hand.

"You're welcome."

He sat next to me on the couch and rested his arms across the top. While I drank the water, he tapped his fingers and patted his foot on the floor.

"Damn, where is she?" he said. "She should've been here by now."

"Who," I said, sitting the glass on the table in front of me. "Your nanny?"

He sat up and quickly removed the glass from the table. "Not there," he said. "Let me get you a coaster."

Jaylin reached for a coaster and then placed the glass on top of it. He sat back again, but this time he crossed one leg over the other. "Yes," he said. "My nanny."

As I was getting ready to respond, the little girl came into the room. Her natural long hair was secured with a pink headband that had a yellow flower on it. The teddy bear remained against her chest and she looked at her father with wide eyes that were the color of his.

"Yes, Jaylene," he said. "What can I get you?"

"I want two cookies and some milk. You said you'd get them for me earlier, but you still haven't gotten them."

Her little sweet, timid voice was heart-warming. Jaylin excused himself. He wasted no time going into the kitchen and honoring his daughter's request.

While he was in the kitchen, Jaylene stood there swaying back and forth with a beautiful smile plastered on her face. "Hi," she said. "My name is Jaylene Rogers. What's your name?"

She was so adorable that I wanted to hold her. I reached out to her, and she came up to me and sat on my lap. "My name is Myra. Myra Walker."

Jaylene tilted her head to the side, inquisitively looking at me. "Myra, are you here to spend some time with *my daddy*?"

I nodded. "Yes, just a little time. He seems like a very nice man, and I would like to get to know him better."

"Hmmm," she said then peeked around me, as if she was looking for someone. She then leaned forward to whisper in my ear. "He is a nice man, but just between us, he only has one leg. The other one is fake."

I cocked my head back and shot her a puzzled look. "A fake leg? Really?"

Jaylene nodded. She then leaned in to whisper in my ear again. "Before my dad comes back, you might want to get that *thing* out of your nose. It's pretty big and green."

I wasn't sure if she was being truthful about something being in my nose or not, especially after the leg thing that definitely wasn't true. Besides that, I didn't like kids who told lies. I quickly removed her from my lap and turned my head in another direction to avoid her. When Jaylin returned to the room, I couldn't help but to examine his legs that were visible from the white shorts he wore.

"Your cookies and milk are on the kitchen table," he said to Jaylene. "Go eat, and do you know where your sister and brothers are at?"

She shrugged and scratched her head. "No, Daddy. I don't know."

Jaylin pat his cheek, and before heading to the kitchen, Jaylene kissed his cheek and thanked him.

He sat next to me on the couch again, and right before his cell phone rang, I asked if I could use the bathroom.

"Sure," he said with the phone in his hand. "It's down the hall over there and to your right."

I got up and hurried to the bathroom, just to be sure there was nothing in my nose. There wasn't, but while I was in the bathroom, I searched the medicine cabinet for condoms and meds. The only thing inside was a bottle of Tylenol and a fingernail file. I closed the cabinet then looked in the mirror to spread more red gloss across my lips. Then I raked my lace-front wig, designed to resemble Beyoncé's hair, with my fingers. The casual pants and shirt I wore fit my petite frame well, and the sandals I had on showed the recent pedicure I'd gotten. I washed my hands, but before I returned to the living room, I walked further down the hallway and peeked into what looked to be a guestroom. It was laid out, and from what I could tell, Jaylin was a man with some serious money. I had to be sure that I played my cards right, because in a matter of time, I was sure he would hook a sista up. When I returned to the living room, he stood, waiting for me.

"Listen," he said. "That call was from my nanny. She ran out of gas on the highway, and I need to go make sure everything is good with her. If you would do me a huge favor and watch my kids for twenty . . . maybe thirty minutes, I would appreciate it. I promise I'll be back as soon as I can."

I hesitated a little, but I guess there was no harm in helping out. Plus, if I was going to be kicking it with him, I needed to meet his kids. "Sure, Jaylin, no problem. Take your time and please make sure your nanny is okay."

Jaylin nodded then hit an intercom button. He yelled into it. "Mackenzie, LJ and Justin, into the living room, pronto. This is an emergency."

Dang, how many kids did he have? Hopefully, they were much older because I wasn't in the mood to be watching a bunch of snotty-nosed kids. I didn't have any children—couldn't have any, as a matter of fact, but my sister's kids were like my own. There were times when I watched all six of them, and being around them drove me nuts.

Minutes later, a tall boy who appeared to be about eight or nine came into the room with a basketball tucked underneath his arm. He was handsome as ever, and a future model was written all over him. Then an older girl with extremely long hair that was midway down her back rushed in, carrying a little boy who made my heart melt once again. Now, I truly felt as if all children were beautiful, but these kids looked magazine ready. From their clothes to their hairstyles, they all had it going on.

"I need to go pick up Nanny B and make sure she's okay," Jaylin said to his kids. "Myra is going to keep good care of y'all while I'm gone, and it will only be for about thirty minutes. Be nice to her and stay out of trouble. If anybody needs me, call me."

The children seemed so polite. They hugged their father and stood by the door as he made an exit. Afterward, they came over to the couch where I was. Jaylene was back with her cookies and teddy bear. She sat directly next to me.

"Myra is here to get to know daddy better," she said to the others. She then introduced them one by one, but they didn't say much, so Jaylene continued. "I already told her about daddy's leg, but I guess she doesn't believe me."

Mackenzie rolled her eyes. "Jaylene, stop telling people that daddy has a fake leg. But what exactly is it that you want to know about our dad?"

Her eyes narrowed as she spoke, and to be honest, I didn't like this little girl's attitude. I knew how some kids were when it came to their parents dating, so I did my best not to trip.

"Nothing in particular, just . . . I just want to become good friends with him."

"He already has enough friends," LJ said then stood to bounce the basketball. The glass on some of the shelves started to rattle, and one of the pictures above the fireplace mantel fell and crashed to the floor.

I snapped my head to the side, almost ready to go off on him. "Uh, you may not want to bounce that ball in here. Why don't you play with that outside?"

"You're not his mother," Jaylene hissed then pointed to her chest. "Because my mom is extra pretty and she looks nothing like you. She looks just like me."

Good for her, I thought. I was taken aback by her snippiness too, but I remained cool, calm and collected. "Maybe she is pretty, but I don't want anything else to break in here. Just cool out, until your father gets back."

I got off the couch to pick up the broken picture frame. It was a picture of the oldest girl with Jaylin. She rushed up to me and took the picture from my hand, ripping it.

"Oh my God," she said, looking down at the picture. "You ripped my picture! I can't wait until *my daddy* gets back here so I can tell him that you ripped our picture!"

I was so annoyed. LJ was still in the background bouncing the ball, and the sound was starting to give me a headache. "I didn't rip your picture. You ripped it, when you snatched it from my hand."

"I did not," she said, raising her voice. "You were jealous and you ripped it."

"Jealous of what?" I snapped.

She stormed away, pouting. I couldn't believe this was happening, and when the basketball crashed into the living room table, breaking the glass, I let LJ have it.

"See, I told you that would happen, didn't I? You should have listened to me, when I told you to go outside with that ball."

To no surprise, he ignored me and kept bouncing the ball. Jaylene slapped her hand over her mouth and pointed to me. She removed her hand then laughed. "Ooooo, you are in deep trouble, and as *my daddy* always says, there will be consequences. He gon' get youuuuu, lady, he is going to spank you so hard!"

I pointed to my chest. "Get me? Get me for what, when your hardheaded brother over there is the one who broke it?"

"My name is LJ. Jaylin Rogers, number two."

Was I being *Punk'd* by Ashton Kutcher or what? Had to be because kids didn't come like this. Yet again, I put LJ in his place.

"I don't give a damn what your name is. You're the one who broke that table and you will be punished for doing so."

They all laughed, including the little boy, Justin, who was walking around with a wet paintbrush in his hand. I was so busy with the other two kids that I didn't notice red paint on the tip of his brush.

"Did I just hear her curse," Mackenzie said, coming back into the room and appearing shocked by my words.

Jaylene confirmed it by quickly nodding like a bobble-head doll. "Yes, she did use the 'd' word and *my daddy* doesn't allow bad words in the house."

For the moment, I ignored them and rushed up to Justin who had already swiped the white sectional with red paint. "Give me that," I said, reaching for the brush in his hand. "How . . . who gave that to you?"

After I took the brush, he carefully dropped to the floor so he wouldn't injure himself, and then cried and threw a tantrum.

"See what you did," Mackenzie said, helping Justin off the floor. "Don't cry, Justin. Let's go call Mama and tell her about this hoodrat over here."

Who in the hell was she calling a hoodrat? Really? They left the room, but LJ stood gazing at me with the ball tucked underneath his arm. "If Scorpio gets here before my dad does, you gon' get beat down. And this is for making my little brother cry."

He lifted the ball over his head and threw it at the flat-screen TV mounted on the wall. The TV screen cracked into several pieces. My jaw dropped and my eyes were wide as saucers. Jaylene cried out, and when I snapped my head to the side to look at her, tears streamed down her face. Her cheeks were beet red and her lips were poked out.

"Look what you did, LJ," she said. "Now I won't be able to watch my cartoons anymore. I can't wait to tell . . . *my daddy*."

LJ pointed to me. "She's the one who made me do it. Don't go blaming me. Blame her."

Obviously, this little girl had a lot of faith in her daddy. Was he all that? She was working my damn nerves, as was the rest of them. With a mean mug on her face, Jaylene came up to me. She lifted her tiny foot, stomping it on mine. I'd be lying if I said it hurt, but since I didn't say anything, she made her teddy bear stomp on my foot too.

"Go home," she said. "We don't want you here, and neither will *my daddy*, once he finds out you did all of this."

What in the hell was wrong with these kids? They were the ones who did all of this crap, and they were not about to blame it on me. I shouted at LJ and Jaylene, as they left the room, hooting and hollering about how much trouble I was in.

"Yeah, well, we'll see about that, won't we?" I said.

I reached for my cell phone to call Jaylin and tell him about these bad-ass kids. Unfortunately, he didn't answer. I was getting ready to leave him a message, until I heard a loud crash coming from the kitchen. I dropped my phone on the couch and ran into the kitchen. Jaylene was at it again; this time in the refrigerator, claiming that she was about to cook lunch. A broken mayonnaise jar was on the floor. I was kind enough to move her away from the glass, so she wouldn't cut her feet.

"All I wanted was a tuna sandwich," she said, staring at me with those tearful, gray eyes. "Why wouldn't you make me one? We're going to starve to death, and *my daddy's* going to be real mad at you for killing us."

"Let go of her arm," LJ said, walking up to me. "You're holding her arm too tight."

By now, I was on edge and couldn't control my attitude. I pointed my finger near his face and encouraged Miss Jaylene to listen up too. "If you wanted something to eat, you should have asked. Now, please do me a favor and go sit the hell down somewhere, before your father gets here. I just called him and he said he's on his way."

"And you believed him," LJ said, laughing. "He's not on his way, nor did he go see what was up with Nanny B."

I was shocked. Did he know something that I didn't? Was this all in Jaylin's plan? I didn't know what the hell was going on, but before I could say anything else, I felt a sharp pain in my toe. When I looked down, I noticed that some of the glass from the Mayo jar had sliced my foot. I bent over to see how deep the cut was, and that was when Jaylene snatched the lace-front wig from my head. She ran off with it, twirling it around and giggling.

"Look! We got another doggy! He's big and furry."

I stood and charged after that little girl. God help her, if I caught up with her. Her ass was mine and I was going to teach her something that her mama and daddy should have taught her.

"Come here, you little—"

Jaylene screamed as I chased her around the house. The whole time, she didn't dare depart with that teddy bear and I couldn't believe how fast she was. I was out of breath as I climbed the stairs to go after her, and when I looked downstairs into the living room, Mackenzie and LJ stood there laughing. Justin was decorating the couch again, and red handprints were everywhere.

"That's it," I said, throwing my hands in the air. "I'm out. Y'all too damn bad for me."

I made my way down the stairs and back into the living room. By then, Mackenzie had my cell phone in her hands, looking through my pictures.

"Yucky," she said. "I hope *my daddy* hasn't seen those naked pictures of you. That's nasty."

"Yo Mama." I snatched the phone from her hand, knowing what kinds of pictures I had on there. I then tucked my purse underneath my arm and limped my way to the door.

"I'm sure you all are old enough to take care of yourselves. Good luck and good riddance!"

"Don't leave without your doggy!" Jaylene said, tossing my wig over the upstairs railing. "Weeeee."

The wig landed on the couch, and realizing how tangled my real hair was, I rushed over to the couch to get my wig. As I reached for it, Justin reached for it too. We played a game of tug-a-war, and I couldn't believe how strong that little boy was.

"No," he shouted, cried and stomped his feet. "Gimmie my doggy back."

"Look, sweetie, this is not a dog. This is mine and I want you to let it go right now."

"She's making him cry again," Mackenzie said. "I wish my mother would hurry up and get here, and *my daddy* will hurt anyone who makes his kids cry."

I was so freaking tired of hearing about their daddy. I surrendered my wig to Justin and turned to Mackenzie. "You know what? Fuck your daddy, okay? This is some B.S.—"

Right after I said that, the door came open and in walked Jaylin. Next to him was an older lady who looked to be in her fifties or sixties. Their eyes scanned the room that looked as if a hurricane had blown through it, leaving behind dabs of red paint.

Jaylin narrowed his eyes to look at me then he started to stroke his goatee—hard. "Fuck me," he said. "You come over here, destroy my house and disrespect my kids, but fuck me?"

Jaylene ran up to him, crying and sobbing as if the world was coming to an end. "She . . . she was mean to us, *Daddy*. And look at what she did to my teddy bear. The one you bought me when I was born."

The teddy bear now had one eye and cotton was busting out from the stomach and ears. I hadn't even touched her teddy bear, but the evil look in Jaylin's eyes let me know that he believed her.

"Uh, to hell with that teddy bear," I said, looking around the room. "Look at what they did to your couch, the TV and your table. I told them—"

"Get the fuck out of here!" he yelled with thick wrinkles on his forehead. "Now! Before I do something I'm going to regret!"

The woman next to him rubbed his back, asking for him to calm down. "It'll be okay, Jaylin. She got one minute to leave, or we'll call the police. You can sue her for the damages later, and I'm sure you will recoup every single dime."

I put my hand on my hip and shook my head. "Seriously, though. Sue me for what? Nigga, these bad-ass kids of yours are the ones who did this and you need to be finding a belt to spank their bleep-bleep-bleep-bleep-bleep!"

The all appeared shocked by my choice of words, but I didn't care. LJ stepped up to Jaylin, shrugging his shoulders. "What have you always told me about ghetto girls with foul mouths and who refer to us as the "n" word? Don't trip, dad. She wasn't your type anyway, and Mom looks waaaay better than she does. Stick with who you got, cause this lady is coo-coo."

I wanted to scream and choke somebody. How did I ever manage to get myself in a situation like this one? The next fine man I saw, I intended to keep it moving.

I ignored everyone else and looked at Jaylin. "This has been a very traumatic experience for me, and I will never, ever reach out to you again." I stormed toward the door, and on my way out, the old woman grabbed me by my arm. She cleared her throat then delivered a forced smile.

"For the record, there's only one woman allowed in this house. You're looking at her, so don't ever come here again, unless I invite you."

I snatched away from her and ran outside to get into my car. Wigless and all, I sped off thinking to hell with Jaylin Rogers and his millions. I wanted no parts of his world, and it was a damn shame that things just didn't work out. I was sure his kids were happy about that.

RIGHT PLACE, WRONG TIME

By Ashley Benton

This never would have happened, had I not been lonely and deprived. While my husband, Chris, thought that money was key to saving our failing marriage, it wasn't. I truly didn't believe that having all the money in the world would turn our situation around. I made that very clear to him, but whenever I mentioned something about our chaotic marriage, he ignored me.

What I wanted was simple. That consisted of a man who catered to me and provided great sex. Since Chris and I hadn't gone there in about three months, I was forced to turn elsewhere. And who would have thought that the man I'd been reading about in books would deliver in a major way. I'd met him while kicking it with some of my friends, and his, on his yacht. The party was off the chain. I was so captured by Jaylin Rogers that I slipped him my number that night. He reached out at the right time, and the rest was history.

I sat back on the bed, holding myself up with my elbows. My butterscotch colored naked body was dotted with numerous beads of sweat. My eyes scrolled down the tall, handsome man that stood before me. His entire body was crafted to near perfection. Abs were stacked with muscles, broad shoulders resembled a linebackers and his delicious, nine-inch dick pointed in my direction. My legs fell apart, and the gates to my moist haven welcomed him. I could already feel my juices flowing through the crack of my ass, even though Jaylin hadn't laid one finger on me. My hairless slit puckered at him, and as I opened my legs even wider, my swollen clit played a few seconds of peek-a-boo. Jaylin's sexy eyes zoned in. His tongue traveled from one corner of his mouth to the other, as he licked his lips. He didn't blink. He didn't move. All he did was stare. I could tell he was hungry for me; I was more than eager to give him something tasteful to eat.

Jaylin inched forward while stroking his heavy meat. He massaged it. Pulled it. Squeezed it and made it grow even longer. Almost immediately, I felt my pussy wanting to erupt like a volcano. It had a slow beat that picked up with every step that Jaylin took forward. As he kneeled on the bed, the room fell silent. My breathing halted. My eyes fluttered and my legs started to slightly tremble. He gave them a soft pat, and then he reached out to examine me. While on his knees, he slipped two of his fingers inside of my heated, sopping wet pussy. He stretched it from left to right, pulling it apart so he could search deeper—deeper with the object of his choice. He lowered his face between my legs, and I could smell my sweet juices infuse the air. He sucked in a deep breath and gazed at me with a Crest smile displayed on his face.

"Your pussy is top notch, baby," he said. "Are you ready for me?"

I slowly nodded. And when his soft lips touched my shaky legs to calm them, my firm breasts rose. A deep arch formed in my back; my stomached tightened. Jaylin planted a trail of soft kisses against my shapely thighs, along my hipbone and against the tip of my slit. As he added pressure with his mouth, I welcomed him inside by spreading my pussy lips. My clit gave him a quick hello, and it wasn't long before he washed his tongue right over it. His circles started off slow. With each second, his tongue picked up great speeds. The arch in my back grew higher. I could feel a blast of heat transpiring from the tips of my toes, all the way to my vagina. It started to make noises. Noises that let Jaylin know how aroused I really was. He backed his tongue away from my pearl and lightly licked it against my folds. I wanted to suck him right in, but he always encouraged me to be patient. Patient I was, until he dipped his velvety tongue further inside, causing me to gasp. My fists tightened, and I sucked my bottom lip into my mouth. Almost in slow motion, I dropped back on the pillow, causing my wavy, long hair to spread all over it. I closed my fluttering eyes and thought about how thankful I was for Jaylin Rogers. He specialized in giving pleasure—that was so obvious by the way he toyed with my insides.

"I love this," I whispered as his tongue journeyed further inside of me. "Right there, Jay Baby, right there!"

He moved beyond there. His tongue traveled deep within, tickling every spot that he touched. I wanted to laugh and cry at the same time. Even thought about jumping for joy, but I didn't dare move away from the amazing feeling that was taking over my body. His tongue slithered in and out of me, as if it were a warm dick. His fingers assisted, and as he gestured them in a come-here motion, my heavy, sweet glaze covered them. He licked my cream from his fingers then inserted them again. His rotations became more rhythmic, more satisfying. I grinded my hips and was unable to lye still from his touch. His thumb brushed against my clit, and within a matter of seconds, I rained on his fingers. I squirted his lips and covered his mouth with a buildup of my excitement.

"More." I was barely able to catch my breath. "Dammit, give me more!"

Jaylin inched away from me and smiled. He was arrogant and confident at the same time. He knew I was a horny bitch, and since I'd reached my first climax, he knew exactly where to venture next.

"Bend over," he said.

I happily turned on my stomach and positioned myself doggy style on my hands and knees. My hair fell over my face and I held my hands together, knowing that he was about to tackle my asshole in a major way. He beat his dick against my butt cheeks, damn near turning them red. He rolled the tip of his mushroom head through my crack to tease me. My heart rate increased again. I was eager for him to fuck me, but he always insisted on teasing me until I couldn't take no more. He massaged his hands over the mountains of my ass, and then spread my cheeks far apart. After wetting his lips, he lowered his head and touched the tip of my crack with his tongue. It traveled south until he reached my asshole. That's where he went into action. His tongue fluttered against it, making my legs shake. I squeezed my butt cheeks to help calm the intense feeling, but it did me no good, especially when he inserted his fingers. One in my pussy, the other in my asshole. My mouth was wide open; I was almost speechless.

"Ahhhhh, ooohhh, ummmmm," I moaned out loudly as my fingernails clawed the sheets. "My poo-say is on fire!"

"Yes, it is." Jaylin wiped across his wet lips. "I feel the fire, and it's definitely hot in that mutha."

His fingers continued in action. I rocked back and forth, trying to keep up with his impressive rhythm. My pussy dripped. Cum ran down my legs and onto the sheets. I screamed as loudly as I could, and the only thing that silenced me was when Jaylin released his fingers and inserted his overly large package. Almost immediately, I clamped my mouth shut and whimpered. My pussy was stuffed to capacity. I could feel every inch of him, sliding in and out of my slippery hole. My folds sunk in with each hard thrust. The bed rocked faster and faster. The intense smell of sex became more prominent, and the room felt hotter than it was before. Jaylin reached for my hair and raked his fingers through it. As his pace increased, his grip in my hair got tighter. He grabbed and pulled—pulled so hard that my head was yanked back. I grunted. Grunted from the feel of his massive dick battering my insides. It felt so good, yet he was being so bad.

"I want this pussy morning, day and night," he confessed. "Portia, I've got to have it."

In the moment, I saw no problem with that whatsoever. As a matter of fact, he was welcomed to it. He could have me in a filthy alley with rats running around, if he wanted. Or in a church where we could both sing hallelujah. That's how badly I craved for this man, and there was no secret that he craved for me too.

He released my hair, giving my neck some relief. My pussy, however, was still being fed as he held my perfect waistline. He squeezed his fingers into my flesh and guided me. My ass slapped against his thighs. I could barely keep up with him, and as sweat dripped from his body, onto mine, I rubbed it all over me. I reached back to touch his ass and could feel his ass muscles tighten with each thrust. His dick began to throb inside of me, and as it expanded, I forced back with a squeeze. He secured the grip on my hips. He halted his movements and released a flood of his semen. I didn't want any of it to go to waste, so I moved forward and hurried to turn around. I covered his dick with my mouth, sucking it in to the back of my throat. The feeling was too intense for him, so he yanked my hair and pulled back.

"I can't," he said nearly out of breath. "Give me a minute . . . maybe two."

I licked some more, but then backed away to let him regroup. That didn't take long, and before we knew it, we took our sexual escapade to the couch where I was bent over it. With my legs straddled wide, he stood behind me. I was on the tips of my toes while his dick rested comfortably inside of me. Soft kisses were planted against my back, and he began to rub my body with oils that made my skin silky and smooth. As his hands roamed my curves, my eyes were shut tight. I was in deep thought about what was happening to me. Never, ever had my pussy been more pleased. He reached around to my slit and began to twist and turn my pearl. As it hardened from his touch, he plunged his dick inside of me. This time, his movements were slow. His thrusts were perfect. My juices sounded off in the room, and his moans grew louder.

"Baby, your pussy is a mind twister. I . . . I can't get enough of it, I swear."

Jaylin pulled out of my pussy and broke into my asshole. I flinched a bit from his abrupt change of plans, but it didn't take long for me to relax. With my asshole now filled, he lifted my legs to his lap and held my waist. He balanced me on his thighs and rocked our bodies back and forth. I didn't anticipate on coming this way, but as his fingers worked magic inside of my kitty, I was on the verge of another explosion.

"Jaaaaylinnnn! Fuck me harder . . . go hard, you sexy motherfucker, go hard!"

He switched up the pace and went harder. We rocked our bodies together so fast that the couch started to move and scratch the hardwood floor. All we could do was laugh. Laugh at how much fun we were having; at how much we enjoyed each other's company. He had given me so much that I had to return the favor. So while he lay back on the couch, I straddled the top of him. His hands traced my curves, and before I could even insert his meat inside of me, his mouth sucked in my breast. I served him a hard nipple, and then inched down on his lengthy muscle that was waiting to break my slit apart again. This time, I paced myself. I took in six inches then seven. After seven I went for eight. I only had one inch left, so I took my time before I slammed all the way down, making his steel reach the depths of my deep tunnel. I put another arch in my back and rode him like I was a jockey. My breasts wobbled faster. My hips grinded harder. My mouth was dropped open, and his dick remained harder than a black diamond. I bounced up and down on him, and he pulled my cheeks apart, making his insertions much easier. For some reason or another, he felt as if my pussy had had enough, so his strokes resumed in my ass. I just couldn't get enough of this man. No matter how long he stroked, I wanted more and more.

Feeling slightly defeated, I dropped forward and rested against his chest. He rubbed my ass then gave it a hard slap.

"I know you're not tired," he said full of energy. "Because now it's time for us to go clean up."

Clean up time was always the best. He reached for my hand and led me to the spacious shower. I turned on the waterfall faucet and we both stood naked underneath it. Jaylin gazed into my eyes and rubbed my hair back with his hands. The direction of his eyes shifted to my lips and we locked in an intense kiss that brought the temperature up a notch. Minutes later, the bathroom began to fill with steam. My hands massaged his body, vice versa. I could feel his dick poking at my midsection, but instead of straddling his waist again, he hit me with another suggestion.

"Grip your ankles and hold on tight."

I honored his request and bent over in front of him. Soothing hot water beat down on my back and I waited patiently for my pussy to be filled again. He toyed with my insides by using the tip of his head to manipulate my hole. I refused to play the waiting game with him, so I threw my ass back and swallowed his muscle in one swoop. He laughed.

"Anxious, are we?"

I responded by spreading my legs wide and letting him sink further inside of me. We carried on like two dogs in heat. Water splashed everywhere, especially when our bodies slapped against each other's. When all was said and almost done, we had moved our way into the kitchen. He pressed against my backside, as I faced the kitchen table.

"I need you," he whispered while placing his lips close to my ear. "I need you for, at least, another hour or so. Tell me your husband isn't coming home anytime soon. If he does, too damn bad."

I agreed . . . too damn bad! Jaylin massaged my breasts together and turned my nipples. I squirmed from the touch of his hands then turned around to face him. We held a long stare, knowing that I was a married woman, and he was, well . . . just trying to keep his dick wet. But there was no shame, whatsoever. This was something that I needed, simply because my significant other had failed me. More than anything, it was a fuck thing for both of us, and we were perfectly fine with it. Still, my eyes watered. Why? Because we had been at this for hours. I knew it was almost coming to an end.

"No emotions," Jaylin said then kissed the corner of my eye where a tear was trying to escape. He didn't want to see me upset, and the truth was, I didn't want him to see me sad. I was elated when he spilled the words "bend over" again.

I poured my body over the glass-topped table, and Jaylin squatted. My hot box stared him right in the face, and he began to take light licks between my legs. Like always, the further he went inside, my legs started to buckle. I sprayed his lips with a small amount of my sweet juices, and as we hurried to the finish line, he kissed my forehead.

"Until next time," he said, towering over my small frame.

"Yes, until next time. My husband should be home late tonight, but I suspect that he'll be back on the road within another day or two. I'll call you, so we can pick up where we left off."

"No doubt," he said then put on his clothes and left. I closed the door behind him and smiled at what I hoped the future would bring.

The next day, I lay in bed, resting rather well. All I could feel were the black, silk sheets sliding off my naked body. Just for a few seconds, I smiled, thinking that Jaylin was in my bedroom. But as I cracked my eyes open and smelled Chris' cologne, I knew it was him. I continued to lie on my stomach, without saying one word. Chris crawled on the bed and lay on top of me. I could feel his warm body that was definitely fit, but not as fit as Jaylin's. His package wasn't as big as Jaylin's either, but since he was my husband, I allowed him to have his way with me. He leaned into my ear, licking around it and nibbling at my lobes.

"Welcome home to me, huh?" he said, referring to my naked body. I guess he figured I was in bed waiting for him to bring me pleasure. He couldn't have been more wrong. But since I didn't feel like arguing with him, I lied.

"Yes," I said with a forced smile. "Welcome home."

I wanted to push Chris off me, especially since I wasn't so sure about what had him hyped. Why was he willing to do this with me, when he hadn't touched me in months? Without complaining, I allowed him to ease in between my legs. He wrapped my long legs around his back, and without delivering any foreplay, he slipped his dick inside of me. I felt every bit of his seven inches, but I'd be lying if I said he hadn't fallen a bit short. He grinded inside of me, and I was kind of surprised that there were a little more juices inside of me to stir.

"This pussy is so fucking wet and juicy," he said while taking deep breaths. "I love it, sweetheart, I swear I love you."

I hated to lie, but since he was, why not? "I love you too, but to be honest, Chris, you know we have some *problems*, don't you?"

"I know, but I don't want to talk about them right now. For now, keep quiet and . . . and do me one huge favor."

I was almost afraid to ask. "What's that?"

"Turn that sweet ass around and let me hit it from the back."

Jaylin *liked* to see my ass in action too, but Chris *loved* it. I didn't mind turning around, because I worked out extremely hard to keep my body toned and near flawless. I also didn't want to see Chris' hideous expressions. He made some very weird faces when we fucked and those faces weren't always appealing.

I moved into position and had sex with my husband for a measly ten minutes. He rolled over in bed, barely able to catch his breath. For him to be a man in great shape, I was surprised that he could never last more than fifteen minutes. This was the main reason why I felt so deprived, and it was why I sought other alternatives. Alternatives that always kept me knocking at Jaylin's door, while my husband was away. I didn't trust him as far as I could see him, and a wife always knew when her husband had been unfaithful. Chris cheated several times, and instead of sitting around the house crying about it, I got even. Not only did I get even, but I found one of the finest men on the planet to give the goodies to. To me, that was Jaylin.

The following morning, I sat at the breakfast table with heavy thoughts. Chris had joined me, but he didn't say much to me. He noticed how quiet I was too, and that was when he finally asked if I had something on my mind. I sipped from my glass of apple juice then placed it on the table.

"As a matter of fact, I do have something on my mind. I have a lot of things on my mind, but I want you to be as truthful with me, as I intend to be with you."

Chris nodded. "I can do that. Now, what's up?"

I didn't dare hold back. "I've said this to you a million and one times before, but I don't think you're listening to me. That is, I'm unhappy. I'm very unhappy and I can't continue to live like this."

"So, what are you saying? Are you finally saying that you want a divorce? I mean, you've never said that before, and I want to be sure that's what you want."

I swallowed the lump in my throat and was unable to answer his question. The truth . . . I wasn't sure what I really wanted. I didn't know if I wanted to keep fucking Jaylin, or if I wanted to somehow or someway work things out with my husband. If I did, he'd have to make some major changes.

"Can I simply say that I'm confused? I'm not sure if a divorce is the right answer, but I definitely know that something needs to change. I'm tired of being alone all the time, and even though you've done a lot to take care of me, it's not enough. I want more. More of you . . . of us. Not having you here is causing me to do things that you may not be happy with. Things that I know will make you hate me, instead of love me."

Chris stroked the hair on his chin and smirked. "I must be honest and tell you that I love and appreciate a woman who confesses her sins and wants to come clean. It took you long enough to say what you just did, and all I can say is it's about damn time. You keep telling me that I'm the one who needs to change, but realistically, aren't you the one who needs to get your act together? You bitch all the time about being alone, but the truth is, you're not alone, Portia. You haven't been alone for quite some time and you can thank Mr. Rogers for that. He gives you what you want, and when I'm not here, you have the audacity to bring that motherfucker in my house, fuck him in my bed and give that bastard head while in my shower. That doesn't include the numerous times that you've fucked him in the car I bought you, nor does it have anything to do with the clothes that I've seen him strip from your body to get to your pussy. Just so you know, I bought those clothes too. With all of that being said, let me make myself clear on one thing. I welcome a divorce, sweetheart, and if you want one, all you have to do is say the magic word. To me, you're not confused. All you are is a greedy little bitch who uses people to get whatever you want from them. There's no doubt that I'm your money maker. And apparently, Jaylin has the dick of your dreams. I'll let you decide which is more important, and whatever you decide, please let me know."

I stared at Chris the whole time without a blink. I couldn't believe that he'd known about Jaylin all of this time and hadn't said a word. I was almost speechless, but I couldn't allow him to dump all of this into my lap and not take *some* responsibility for our failing marriage.

"So you know about my lover, now what? He wouldn't be the dick of my dreams, had you been serving me the right way. I don't know what you expect for me to do, other than for me to sit in this damn house all day, eating chocolates, watching reality TV shows and playing with myself. That gets tiresome. If I've found someone who brings a little excitement to my life, so be it. You weren't doing anything, and all you think about is money, money, money. That's who you love—money. Well, money can't buy you love, sweetheart. Money can't bring you happiness and neither can I, under these conditions. But since you're always gone and on the phone with whomever, maybe you have found someone who you can love, more than your freaking money."

Chris made my eye twitch when he laughed at my comment. "You're getting desperate," he said. "You can't try to flip the script, and trust me when I tell you that I so wish that I had someone to love, more than I do money. You are so right about that—I do love my money. Why? Because it gives me power. It's going to give me all the power I need to fight you in court and make sure you don't get one single dime of my money when I leave you. It's going to leave you broke . . . out in the streets with no damn place to go. I have a visualization of that day, and I can't stress enough how delighted I will be when I get rid of you."

I'd heard enough of this bullshit. How dare he speak to me this way? What in the hell was in his juice this morning that made him take this thing to a whole new level? I backed away from the table and dabbed my mouth with a napkin. I walked to his side of the table and stood next to him.

"If a battle in court is what you want, trust me, you'll get it. Don't underestimate me, and you are a fool if you believe your money gives you power. Power comes from within, and when a person feels as though their back is against the wall, you'd be surprised by who or what shows up. In the meantime, thanks for the shitty breakfast. I have some shopping to do, and I may stop by my lover's place to see what's up with the dick of my dreams. So, don't wait up for me tonight. There's always a possibility that I won't be coming home."

I splashed Chris' face with apple juice and stormed away. He laughed and clapped his hands.

"You're brilliant, Portia! Fucking brilliant, yet you're still one dumb bitch!"

His words cut me like a sharpened knife, but I didn't respond. Why? Because I knew that in the end, I'd be the real winner.

Later that day, I was feeling down in the dumps. That was until I had gone to see an attorney who had given me hope. I was about to leave Chris high and dry. He just didn't know it yet, but soon enough this marriage would be over and I would be a free woman. I wanted to share my good news with Jaylin. Even though I knew he wasn't down with dating anyone on a serious level, still, we had become good friends. I loved to talk and he loved to listen. I believe that he truly wanted what was best for me, but I had to want the best for myself first.

I parked my car on the parking lot where Jaylin lived. I saw him getting out at the same time and approached him.

"I know it's wrong of me to show up without calling," I said. "But I had to see you."

"It's okay," he said, opening his arms to give me a hug. "It's been a long day, anyway. And what a sight for sore eyes you are."

He always knew the right things to say to me. "Same here," I said as we walked toward the elevator that would take us to his loft. "By the way, why haven't you answered your phone all day? I tried to call you."

"Been busy, baby. That's all."

Jaylin displayed a crooked smile. He knew what was in the works for him this evening, and the second we got on the elevator, he wasted no time pulling me into his arms. Leaving no breathing room between us, he tightened his arm around my waist then lowered it to my ass. He gave it a tight squeeze, and then dug underneath my short skirt to venture elsewhere.

Thankfully for the both of us, I was wearing a thong. He slipped the crotch section aside with his finger, trying to sink it into my wetness.

"No," I said, backing away from him. "Not yet. You're the one who needs this, more than me."

Jaylin didn't put up a fuss. I dropped to my knees and started to unzip his pants. The hard hump that was already there made it difficult, but I was able to roll the zipper over his dick that had grown to new heights. I yanked his pants down to his knees, and licked my lips at his dick that plopped out long, thick and hard. His back was against the wall, and before I slipped his dick into my mouth, he hurried to remove his pants. He straddled his legs and held his full package close to my rosy-red lips.

"Do your thing, baby. Proceed."

I opened my mouth wide and proceeded, as he'd told me. He pumped my mouth like it was a throbbing pussy. I used one hand to massage his sticky balls and the other hand I used in action with my mouth. His dick was very tasteful, and as his veins became more visible, I drove my mouth into overtime. He squirmed against the wall with bunches of my hair tightened in his hand.

"You damn sure know how to relieve a man's stress," he said. "And there I was thinking aspirin would do the job."

I wanted to laugh, but couldn't because my mouth was full. I kept bobbing my head, but when the doors to the elevator opened, I quickly pulled back and snapped my head to the side. On the other side was an older woman with wide eyes that looked as if they were about to break from her sockets. Again, I wanted to laugh, but couldn't.

"The two of you have the right idea, but . . . but you're doing it in the wrong place. I'm in a hurry. I need to get to my car."

I was so sure that Jaylin would know how to handle this, but he hadn't said one word. I, however, took the initiative to settle this little setback.

I stood and held on to his steel to keep it hard. My mouth was wet, so I licked my lips and smiled at the lady.

"Sorry for the inconvenience, but we're on our way up. You're going down, and in a few more minutes, the elevator will return. I promise."

I hit the up button to make the elevator close. I could have sworn that the old woman called me a trifling bitch, but I didn't have time for her right now. I resumed my business with Jaylin, and by the time we reached his floor, we were ripping each other's clothes off. He pushed me against his door and ran kisses up and down my neck. One of my legs was hiked up while he grinded his hardness against me. My pussy throbbed. I wanted him to fuck me so badly, but unfortunately, he wrestled with the keys as he tried to unlock the door.

Seconds later, the door busted wide open and slammed against the wall. Jaylin lifted my other leg and straddled me against his midsection. He carried me into his office, where there was a small desk that had many papers on top of it. In one swipe, he made the papers hit the floor and cleared the desk. He positioned his dick right at the crevasses of my cream-filled pocket and rolled it around. The sounds of my juices were like music to our ears. The melody came across loud and clear, especially when Jaylin slammed inside to make my cherry burst. I dropped my head back and looked up at the ceiling. Damn this man felt good inside of me. It was as if he was destined to be there. This was exactly what I wanted in my life, and I kept telling myself to hell with Chris. The way Jaylin was fucking the hell out of me, I would never let him go.

With him holding my legs and straddling them far apart, we both kept our eyes focused on his insertions. His dick dripped wet from my fluids, and every time it disappeared in my hole, I gasped. I wanted to cry out. I wanted to holler and scream. Hell, I wanted to tell him how much I loved the way he fucked me, but I couldn't say one word. My tongue was tied, especially when I turned my head to the right and saw my husband standing there. Jaylin was so engrossed into what had been transpiring between us that he hadn't noticed. He hadn't witnessed the twisted look on Chris' face, I did. His eyes were cold. His lips quivered and his fists were tightened. Me? I really didn't care, because I was on the verge of an orgasm that was about to bring down the house. My screams would've done just that, but I couldn't release one word. Nothing, because when Chris grunted, Jaylin's thrusts had ceased. He followed the direction of my eyes, and that was when his eyes connected with Chris standing in the doorway. Almost immediately, Jaylin dropped my legs. He eased out of me, and as his dripping-wet dick stood at attention, all I could say to Chris was, "Sorry."

He didn't say one word. All he did was raise his hand that carried a 9MM Glock pistol. Jaylin rushed to protect me, and when my husband pulled the trigger, the bullet whistled through the air and landed in the center of Jaylin's chest, busting it wide open. He fell backwards and crashed on top of me as we both hit the floor. His bloody hands trembled over the wound to his chest, and as I watched him fight to catch his breath, I screamed at the top of my lungs. In a panic, Chris dropped the gun and tried to rush away. By then, I scrambled away from Jaylin and made my way to the gun. I didn't think twice, before I pulled the trigger and let my husband have it. His body dropped right at the door, and I crawled back over to Jaylin with the phone in my hand. The 911 operator answered.

"A friend of mine has been shot!" I shouted into the phone. "Please, please hurry! I don't want him to die! If he does, I am one dead bitch! Please hurry!"

I dropped the phone and continued to hold Jaylin in my arms. I added pressure to his chest, doing my best to slow down the bleeding. He was still alive, and I prayed like hell that the paramedics would get here soon. I felt horrible for putting him in this predicament, and even though I was in the right place, it was definitely the wrong time. Unfortunately for me, his breathing slowed . . .

GO DEEPER SO I KNOW IT'S REAL

Shelia B.

Laughter surrounded us as we sat in the lobby of the new hotel we had transferred to, discussing a story we opted to write for a new book, *If Only for Another Night*. The story was supposed to revolve around Jaylin Rogers from Brenda Hampton's Naughty Series. We definitely had something to work with, because we'd gotten to know Jaylin on a different level. In the past, we shared some of our personal business with him, vice versa. At first, I was hyped about writing my story, but then I thought about what an asshole Jaylin could be at times. I predicted that he would disapprove of my story, but a part of me didn't care. The other problem I had was writer's block. I hadn't been able to complete a story in months. My publisher had been inquiring about my next manuscript, and I was trying my best to finish.

If anything, I was exhausted. After arriving in Baltimore for a book signing with fellow author, Oasis, my other writing buddy and close friend and I had checked into a hotel that surely should have been sued for false advertising. We'd wanted to get a hotel close to the venue as possible. Since we'd be depending on someone else for transportation, we were trying to be cognizant of their time. It had turned out to be the biggest mistake of our trip.

The red, dingy carpet looked to be stained with some kind of brown liquid as we made our way down the hall to the elevator, which smelled like mold and mildew. While the room was clean, it says a lot about what we thought of the place, since my friend had sprayed our bed linen down with Lysol. We tried not to let it get us down too much, especially me. I'd gotten my flight cancelled and got to the hotel around midnight. It had been a long day for me so I tried not to complain too much and just be grateful for a safe flight.

We did the first signing at the Essex County Library with no problems. While we didn't have people lined up and down the entryway waiting to see us and get their books signed, we had a nice turn out. The people were fun and lively. They asked questions, some bought books, and at the end of the day, we were happy with the turn of events. What we weren't happy about was going back to that hotel room.

Needless to say, after a roach bigger than my hand chased me and my friend from our room, we called it quits and found a hotel better suited to our needs. The Hilton Baltimore near the BWI Airport was a much better option.

So there we sat in the spacious and bright hotel lobby. The grey and cream linoleum flooring near the check-in desk was spotless. Square light fixtures hung from the ceiling. Grey, cream, and golden accessorized furniture matched wonderfully with the setting, giving the bar and sitting area a lounge type appeal. Fourplay's "After the Dance" wafted through the air and I was all smiles. It felt good to be out of Georgia. And it felt even better to get a good laugh in with my friend.

She was a beautiful woman. Golden skin with minimal makeup. Long auburn hair that cascaded midway down her back. Coffee colored eyes that sparkled, even when she wasn't smiling. She was a full-figured diva who wore her clothes well and carried her weight just the same. Anytime she smiled or laughed she lit up the room. Today, she was dressed in all black. Wide-leg dress pants and a collared button-down blouse that accentuated her waist and breasts. Flat black shoes adorned her feet while the silver bangles, earrings, and necklace set her ensemble.

Years ago, we'd met at the Book Expo of America, and she and I had formed a friendship. She had also been there for me when my whole world came tumbling down a little over a year ago. That was something I didn't care to think about.

"Shelia, you can't pick out the hotel rooms no more, girl. Had us up in Hotel Hell," my friend cajoled.

I gave a hearty laugh. "Now you know you picked that place."

She gave a laugh of her own. "Whatever the case, we're never going back. Don't know what the hell they had going on up in there."

"The pictures online looked nothing like the actual thing. Then they had the nerve to boast free breakfast. It should've been free, especially since the cook was stocking Corn Flakes that were not even Kellogg's."

"Shit looked like the Bates Motel. I expected Norma and Norman to come chasing us down the hall with Dylan standing at the other end trying to shoot us any minute," she joked.

The pictured she'd painted was a funny one and I couldn't help but crack the hell up. We said a few more comical things about the place we'd chosen to stay. Laughed about the hookers we'd seen in the hall. One looked like RuPaul and the other Dennis Rodman. Suffice it to say, we were having a good laugh at our own expense. It wasn't until her phone rang that we calmed down on the laughter.

She picked up her phone and I glanced around a bit. Did some people watching to bide the time. Saw a drunk white man feeling his wife or girlfriend up as they stumbled toward the elevator. Looked over and saw a group of Ques downing shots. Knew they were Ques because of the branded symbol on their biceps. Murmurs of talking, giggling, and raucous laughter lit up the area. It didn't bother me though. As long as I was out of that other hotel, I was fine.

"She's sitting right here," I heard my friend say.

I turned my attention back to her and whispered, "Who's that?"

She just smiled then shook her head. "Bye," she said to whomever was on the phone. "I'm not fooling with you and I'm not telling her that," she fussed.

She moved the phone from her ear, tapped the screen to end the call then looked over at me.

I asked again, "Who was that?"

"Your other friend," she answered then picked up her drink to take a sip.

I rolled my eyes. "Let me guess . . . Jaylin?"

"Ah-huh."

I was curious. "What could he possibly want you to tell me?"

She licked her lips as she laughed. "You know how many times he's invited you to his house and you keep turning that man down."

"Oh, God, here we go. He still isn't used to a woman telling him no I see," I quipped.

"He said you can kiss his ass and he won't be inviting you again."

I flipped my hand. "He'll be okay."

"You know you pissed that man off, Shelia."

I shrugged nonchalantly and took a sip of my dirty Martini.

"I'm almost certain Jaylin isn't fazed by me not taking up his invitation for a visit."

Her brows furrowed and she cast a look at me that said she didn't understand the method to my madness.

"I mean, why say no, Shelia? Last time he came to Atlanta, I heard you two became very acquainted with one another."

"Lies. All lies. Don't believe none of it."

She laughed heartily. "Yeah, okay. You still don't have to keep turning that man down like that."

Sometime during our banter, a few of the Ques came over and introduced themselves. They were all cute in some way, but because I had no interest in having one-night stands or having interludes with married men, their flirting was useless. Still, it was fun to have them try to convince me and my friend to come party with them. The whole time they were there, all I could keep thinking about was how many times I'd turned down Jaylin's invite to come to his house whenever I was in St. Louis.

I knew it seemed like a silly thing, especially since the last time I saw him in Atlanta, he and I did have a pretty interesting time. He'd been interested in purchasing property there. At the time, a time when Jaylin's World was alive and well on Facebook, I wasn't even sure the man was real. Then, one day, he showed up just as he told me he would. After picking my face up from the floor, I was his chauffeur for the day. Drove him to various meetings for his house hunting then, eventually, we ended up in his hotel room.

That was disastrous at first. From throwing insults to throwing drinks in each other's faces, it was all bad. That was until he introduced me to nine inches of pleasure and the sixty-nine ways he could give it to me. Shit, at that time, what he was giving me was needed. I was going through a rough patch in my marriage and he was a welcomed distraction. He knew it too. So I assumed what he'd given me was a pity fuck. Please hold the judgments.

As the night progressed, the Ques gave up since neither my friend nor I were budging. We ordered ourselves a round of wings and fries. Everything was going well, even with her texting on her phone most of the time.

"Still talking to Jaylin?" I asked after the bartender had taken our plates.

She chuckled and said, "I'm talking. He's cursing me out."

"Why?"

"Because he's an asshole."

There was something akin to humor in her eyes as she spoke. There was also a slick smirk on her lips.

"When's the last time you seen Jaylin?"

"You know it's been a while since I've seen him. He's been in one of his moods lately."

"Still the same Jaylin."

"Girl, yeah. Nothing has changed."

A devilish thought formed in my mind. It brought a huge grin to my face.

"What, Shelia?" she said. "Spill it."

"Nothing. Just wondering how you let all that go."

She knew what I was talking about. I suspected that she and Jaylin had been something like a couple at one time or another. But I felt as if she had been keeping their past a secret because she was married.

"I never had it to let go. Besides, I'm married."

I shrugged. "And?"

She frowned and moved around in her seat like she was getting uncomfortable.

"And, I'm not trying to go there with Jaylin."

"Again?"

"You know what, Shelia, I'm not doing this with you tonight."

"Well, yeah, because I'm not Jaylin," I cajoled.

She laughed, but didn't comment further on what I'd said.

"You will not get me to walk into that snare." I was about to say something snarky, but she kept talking. "And you need to worry about what story you're going to submit for this new *If Only for Another Night* book."

"I have nothing else to write about. As a matter of fact, I decided that I don't want to even plague my mind with thoughts of that man."

She glanced behind me, probably looking over at the rest of the Ques making all the noise behind us.

"Damn, why?"

I shrugged. "I just don't. Tackling Jaylin is like trying to tackle a giant at the fifty yard line. You either get him or you don't. You either play by his rules or he won't let you play. And quite frankly, I don't have it in me to stomach anymore of his arrogance than I have to."

"You know he's going to be looking for a story from you, Shelia."

"Well, you can tell him to kiss my ass, because I ain't gon' do it."

She cleared her throat and then averted her eyes before they settled back behind me. The hairs on the back of my neck stood up. The women at the bar and the ones in my immediate vicinity all seemed to turn in my direction. Judging by the hungry looks in their eyes, something or someone had captured their attention. I considered myself a pretty smart person so it didn't take much for me to figure out someone was behind me. Judging by how the women in the place had started to all but gravitate in my general direction, it was safe to assume I knew who was behind me, too.

I glared at my friend. She smiled at me.

"I think you can tell him all that yourself," she quipped.

I slowly turned in my seat. There he stood. Narrowed gray eyes, curly cropped hair that had been tapered to perfection. Square chiseled chin that was decorated with a perfectly aligned goatee. He had golden tint to his skin that seemed to be attracting women like bees to honey. On his wrist sat his signature Rolex. Diamonds accentuated the time device. He was dressed down. Not in his signature Brooks Brothers attire. Still, it was clear to see the short sleeved black polo style shirt had been tailored to hug the muscles in his chest and arms. The tan dress slacks he had on had been outfitted for him as well. It took everything in me not to look at the obvious print of his dick. Seemed like I was the only one though. The other women in the room had no shame. On his feet were black loafers. The whole assemble clearly set him apart from the other men in the room. That wasn't so much because of the outfit itself, but because of how he wore it. No man should be able to wear something to overtly simple and make it look like it had been designed for the gods.

Or it could have been the fact that he stood there with an air that said he owned the moment. Even his posture showed his arrogance.

With one hand in his pocket and the other holding a leather carrying case, he stood regal. Broad shoulders that made him appear larger than life as he gazed down at me with a look of disinterest.

"For some reason, you're always inviting me to kiss your ass like it's something I would enjoy doing," he spat. "How about you kiss my ass? I'm sure both of us would enjoy that more."

I sighed loudly. Had been having a battle of the wits with the man since he and I first met. I was really in no mood to do it in that moment, but there would be no way he would tell me to kiss his ass and that would be that. Even if he did look like he had just walked off a GQ cover photo shoot, none of that had ever mattered to me when he decided to go there with me.

"I'm sure you have enough women kissing your ass, Jaylin. It wouldn't be you if you didn't make a woman feel like she was lucky to even be in your presence. However, I'll pass. I've seen road kill that had a more appetizing appeal."

I gave a snide smirk. I had to wonder just what in the hell he was doing in Baltimore at the exact hotel we were in. That brought my attention back to my friend.

I asked her, "You knew he was here, didn't you?"

"You can say that."

He wanted to know, "You have a problem with me being here?"

I ignored him and asked my friend, "Why is he here?"

She had a smile on her face that told me some sneakiness was afoot. "Had some business to handle. He was on his way somewhere else and decided to touch down and drop off something."

"Uh-huh," I answered.

I watched as Jaylin strolled around the table. He adjusted his pants before taking a seat. He sat like he had no worries, not a care in the world. Laid his carrying case on the table next to him. He took his time ordering, once the waiter walked over to ask him what he wanted.

"Make sure it's top shelf. Don't bring me any off-brand watered-down shit or your tip will reflect my dissatisfaction."

I sucked my teeth and rolled my eyes. My friend shook her head. The waiter nodded with a smile then walked off. Jaylin was known to only take the finest of things in life. So the fact that he was even in the Hilton was surprising to me. Why, you may ask? Jaylin had told people he didn't even know what the store Big Lots was. He was known to not even want to step foot on the property of lesser known hotels. So his exorbitant behavior and 'I'm better than you' attitude wasn't new to me.

I sat silently as he and my friend talked about his vacation to Italy. While they went back and forth, the waiter brought his drink over. After taking a few sips, he leaned over to my friend and said something that only the two of them could hear. Whatever it was caused her to blush red. She shook her head, again, as she crossed her legs. I could tell my friend was just as turned on by the man's antics, as she was annoyed.

"You are so full of shit," she told him. "If that were true, you wouldn't have dissed me that time."

"You hold grudges for years. Can't a man make a mistake?"

"Not one like that."

"So, you don't miss us?"

She looked at him pointedly, "I miss you as a friend, yes. But you and I both know what you're offering comes with stipulations I can't deal with."

I looked on curiously. Was Jaylin trying to woo her *again*? He was the only man I knew who could tell one woman about another and the other woman would still be at his beck and call. Even when he would give his ass to kiss, women still came crawling back. My friend had been one of two who appeared to not give in to him. Then again, my suspicions about them grew, every time we all got together. I found it all comical, so I chuckled lightly. I knew what it was to be a woman fighting the obvious attraction to the man.

"What's so funny?" Jaylin asked me.

"You. You're so not used to a woman saying no or walking away that you don't know what to do with yourself," I answered then picked up my watered-down Martini to take a sip.

His face was stoic. I could garner his reaction.

"Oh. Thought you may have been laughing at the fact your husband had finally left you."

My spine stiffened. Eyes clouded over as they turned to slits. He smirked. I shot daggers at him with my eyes.

"What are you talking about?"

"You must have been a horrible wife to make the man just leave you like that."

"You have no idea what you're talking about. So why don't you shut up?"

"Now, why would I do that? Figured I could speak on the ins and outs of your marriage like you so diligently did mine whenever you saw fit. So tell me something," he inquired with furrowed brows as he leaned forward. "How does it feel?"

I bristled as my mood continued to sour. "How does what feel?"

"How does it feel to have your husband walk away? I find the shit comical, actually. You know, kind of like you did when Nokea walked away from me."

"You were a cheating asshole who didn't know what you had until it was gone."

"I knew what I had, which is why I fought so hard to keep it."

I smirked. "You're right. But you wouldn't have had to fight so hard to keep it if you would have just done right in the first place. You knew what you had, but you just didn't expect her to walk away, did you?"

Jaylin gave a rare chuckle then sat back. "Now, look at this," he said then looked at my friend, who had smartly remained mute during the whole thing, like Beyoncé did when Solange was kicking Jay-Z's ass. "I knew what I had and fought to keep it. She knew what she had and still tried to fight to keep it. One of us is smart and the other is stupid. Nokea was one of the best things that ever happened to me. Shelia's husband has always been an asshole. Yet she stayed and waited until he left, instead of leaving his ass a long time ago." He turned back to me. "You knew he wasn't shit."

The drink in my hand started to shake. I had a good inkling to toss the shit in his face, but judging by the way his brow raised and the way he glanced down at his drink, it would be safe to assume that I'd have a face full of his drink too. I remembered the last time I threw a drink in his face. He'd returned the favor and tossed his back in mine. My eyes watered at the thought of the burning sensation that sent me blindly rushing to the bathroom to wash my eyes with cold water.

Penniless. Husbandless. Loveless. Careless. And damn near homeless. That was what my life had turned out to be after my husband decided to pack up and run off with the nineteen-year-old girl he had been cheating on me with. Did I know he was a nothing-ass Negro when I married him? Not really. Did I know he would run off and leave his kids while he chased random pussy clear to an island in New York named Staten? No. If anything, that was the one thing he'd done in the whole situation that caught me completely off guard. So Jaylin could fuck off. While I knew he'd only been paying me back for the countless times I'd passed judgments on his relationships, it still didn't take away the bitterness left in my mouth from his taunting. I excused myself and walked outside to catch some fresh air.

"Jaylin, why did you do that?" I heard my friend ask as I walked away.

I didn't hear his answer, as I had rushed through the sliding doors of the exit as fast as I could. The night air chilled me as I only had on a sweater. I took a look at my reflection in the glass. To be pissed off, I looked pretty upbeat, which was surprising. Usually when Jaylin and I went tit for tat, I was left with a scowl and the urge to pour hot grits on his dick. My jet black curly hair blew around in the wind. I was still a plus-sized diva myself, but just like my friend, I, too, carried my weight well and wore my clothes just the same. Black tights, a black and white sheer top that fishtailed in the back, and black and white wedged sneakers. I pulled my sweater tighter then took a seat on one of the wrought-iron benches in the front of the place. Cars passed back and forth as valets took keys and handed out numbers. Drunken and loud guests walked in and out of the hotel. The wind blew and slapped me in the face a couple of times.

Maybe the reason you don't look upset is because you know Jaylin is telling the truth, my conscience whispered to me. I sighed and shook my head. I hated to admit, but it was the truth. The man I'd married had shown me time and time again that I wasn't where he wanted to be. I chose to ignore it for the sake of the children. I didn't want to be a single black mother so I chose to stay until he made me a single black mother anyway.

Exactly, so why are you out here sulking? I'm cold, bitch, my conscience roared again. I shook my head and decided to walk back in the building. Besides, letting Jaylin know he had gotten to me would surely make him more arrogant than he was already. So I put on my best *fuck-you* face and decided to not let the man see me sweat.

A few hours later, after he and my friend wrapped up their conversation, she and I made our way back to the tenth floor to our room. The new room we were in was much better. Two pillow-top queen-sized beds. A forty-inch flat-screen TV sat atop the wood grain dresser against the wall. Next to that was a desk with two chairs. The big bay window had the curtain drawn closed with a chair next to it. The light blue carpet was clean and the room smelled fresh. We'd had a long day and even longer night. So we chatted for a bit. She made a few comments about me and Jaylin always verbally fighting. Our war of words had become famous in some settings. I chuckled to myself at the thought. After a while, I'd gotten in bed. Didn't take long for the alcohol to lure me into the land of snoring.

At first, I thought I had been dreaming. A woman's sensual moans serenaded me. I saw Jaylin's face then cursed myself for still having freaky thoughts about the man, even after he'd insulted me. I cursed him in my dreams then turned over to try to go back to sleep. I couldn't, that was how I knew I wasn't dreaming and what I witnessed was real. The muscles in his back coiled like steel cables while succulent thighs wrapped around his waist.

"Jaylin, we can't do this in here," I heard.

"Why not?"

"Shelia's in here."

"So. She already knows what this is."

That gave me pause. So he would just fuck another woman in my presence? Even in my dreams, Jaylin was an asshole. In the flesh, he was one too. The fact that he would be fondly massaging another woman's breasts and kissing her neck while I was in the room showed that he didn't care that he had an audience.

That woman, whoever she was, moaned again. Her auburn hair fell haphazardly around her shoulders. The night shirt she had on was in a messy heap around her waist. Jaylin still had his tan dress slacks on, but obviously that wasn't hindering him. He was mid-stroke when the woman's thighs started to quake.

I had gone from being annoyed that he was sexing another woman with me in the same room, to being curiously intrigued about how he was handling her. When he dipped his knees and scooped her from the table beside the TV, then brought her to the bed I was lying in, my eyes widened. *Damn, a front row?* I thought. The woman was beyond the throes of ecstasy. Jaylin pulled back after laying her down. His dick was hard and purposefully aimed through his zipper and soaked. He unbuckled his belt. Next came the button on his slacks then his pants came down revealing powerful thighs. If it could be possible, he'd gotten even more toned with muscle from the last time I saw him.

Jaylin's abs clenched as he kneeled down and brought his lips to the woman's swollen vaginal lips. There was a wedding band on her finger. As I sat up, the woman grabbed a pillow and tried to hide her face. I was so caught off guard by the whole thing, it took me a minute to close my mouth from the shock of seeing my friend's face. While Jaylin showed his expert skill in the art of cunninglingus, she was either trying to hide her embarrassment or the love faces she was making with the pillow. Either way, Jaylin didn't like that she was covering her face, so once he came up for air, he frowned. Snatched the pillow away from her face and swiftly entered her with a hard thrust.

My mouth was in the permanent shape of an 'O'. He gripped her wrists. Held her hands above her head while he pushed in and out of her. I didn't know what was more interesting . . . the fact that her moans had started to get deeper, more sensual, and louder, or the fact that I was actually watching it all go down.

Jaylin had a determined look on his face. The kind that said a man was intent on bringing a woman the pleasure she would never know from another man. The muscles in his arms flexed as he peered down at her.

"Bet you won't wait this long again to give me some pussy," Jaylin taunted her. "I can tell by how tight it is, somebody ain't been hitting it right," he kept on.

"I hate you so much," she responded.

He bit down on his bottom lip, dipped his hips, and caught the motion of her rising hips. I could tell that even though my friend was fighting to keep control of her senses, she, too, was giving the man with the back arching deep stroke a run for his money.

He grunted. "I like this kind of hate. Keep hating me. Pussy is better when you put a little hate in it."

As bad as I wanted to stay in the bed and keep looking, I felt that I should, at least, get up. And so I did . . . well, I tried to. Jaylin grabbed my ankle.

"Where you going?" he asked.

"Err . . . giving ya'll some space. Looks like ya'll need that," I murmured.

It was the best answer I could come up with. To be honest, I was hoping that maybe I could get to the bathroom where I'd hidden my Hitachi wand and stave off some of the swollen moist heat pooling between my thighs. I'd watched plenty of porn, but what was happening before me was anything but porn. It was live action erotica and something about it tickled my fancy.

To make matters worse, I didn't know how to feel after seeing my friend spread eagle, pussy wet, nipples hardened, breast swollen . . . all in the name of Jaylin Jerome Rogers. Every time Jaylin stroked in and out of her, the sight of his creamy wet nine inches—looked to be more now—made me tense.

Jaylin yanked my thighs, pulling me down to the edge of the bed. Now, I probably could have prevented that, you know. But somewhere deep within the recesses of my dick-deprived, pleasure-starved mind, I really didn't think I wanted to. He let one of my friend's wrists go. His big hand snaked up my thighs. Since I'd only had on some ass-crack riding boy shorts and a sports bra, it didn't take much for his fingers to pull them to the side.

"I always knew you had another side to the freak in you. Seeing my dick in her made you wet, huh?" He teased.

While he taunted, his fingers slid between the folds of my pussy, then slipped inside of me. It had been so long since I'd had anything from a man inside of me that all it took was one come-here motion with his fingers to get me going. It was my turn to be embarrassed. I wanted to reach for a pillow to cover my face, but all I had were my hands. While they covered my face, my hips rolled against his fingers involuntarily. It was the effect of an oncoming orgasm.

The pad of his thumb circled my clitoris and I all but passed out at the sensation. One of my hands left my face to grab his wrist. He snatched his wrist from my hold.

"You want me to stop?" he asked.

God knew I didn't. So against my better judgment, I shook my head.

"No," I answered.

"I wasn't talking to you," he said.

I opened my eyes to see that he had my friend caged between his arms. I fought off my embarrassment and watched on in anticipation of him fingering me again. But it was clear by the scowl on my friend's face that Jaylin's teasing ways was about to get him hit. She was on the brink of an orgasm. It was evident by the way she kept trying to move her hips. However, Jaylin had placed his hands on them to stop her movement. He was controlling the moment, was controlling her. He held her orgasm for ransom and there was little she could do about it.

"Jaylin, you need to stop playing," she stammered.

"No, you need to stop playing with my dick. Why you keep denying me what we both know we want?"

"Because I'm married."

I guess he didn't like that answer. He gave her a swift short stroke that made her eyes roll to the back of her head. She made an ugly come face. All women knew what that was. That was the face we made when a man had hit the right spot. It was sweet torture. Painful pleasure. That point between insanity and death. *Le petite mort.*

"You're married now, right? But whose dick is inside of you?"

"You're not playing fair."

"I'm not playing to be fair. I'm playing to win."

He stood up straight, pushed my friend's knees back until they touched her ears and proved that he was indeed playing to win. He pushed in and out of her, worked his hips like a man who had island in his blood. Shamefully—I'm lying—unabashedly, I watched as she coated his dick in her satisfaction. She glazed him over while he used his sex to get his point across. The veins in his arms sat out strong, muscles strained against the pressure he put on them. He'd worked up a sweat. Skin glistened in the dimly lit room as he cupped her thighs in the crease of his elbows, lifted her supple ass from the bed and made her cry out to the sex gods. If anybody had been in the rooms next to us, they heard it all.

I crossed my thighs and rubbed them together to try to ease the mounting pressure between them. I was jealous as fuck. Wanted to push my friend's ass out the way to quench my thirst, but was certain she would probably fight me if I took an inch away from her orgasmic bliss. My nipples were achingly hard. Breasts had swelled in my sports bra, making the fabric uncomfortable against my areolas. I plopped them from my bra to give reprieve. Took my left breast into my hand and squeezed for dear life.

Jaylin was about to come. It was easy to see by the way his hands had gripped her thighs and by the way his nails were digging into her skin. She was breathing erratically. Jaylin was sucking in short breaths. And meanwhile, I was a fly on the wall trying to figure out why I was in the room in the first place.

"Jesus fucking Christ," she cried out. "Ohmigod. Fuck."

"You like that?"

She gave him a smoldering look. "Go deeper so I know it's real, Jaylin."

I wondered if Jaylin's dick was swelling, getting harder by the minute. Possibly, longer by the second as his release crawled up his spine. His ass muscles had clenched. Thighs were working overtime. Why couldn't the sex gods look down on me? Like my prayers had been answered, one of Jaylin's hands fondled my left breast then slid down to urge me to open my thighs. A thumb aggressively massaging my clit and two fingers deep, he finger fucked me while long dicking my friend. While dick would have been ideal, his fingers were getting the job done. I came so hard; I think I pulled a muscle in my thighs. I couldn't relax. Was tensed up from the built-up pressure. And there was something about seeing Jaylin's head fall back, while my friend threw his thrusts back at him, that had me mentally humming Jill Scott's "Crown Royal on Ice" when he released his satisfaction all over her thighs.

Two orgasms and a nut later, my friend was in the bathroom talking to her husband. Jaylin was sprawled out on my bed, naked as the day he came into the world. I stared at his dick, wondering if it still had life in it. It lay thick against his golden thighs.

"Stop staring at my dick," he jibed.

"I wasn't."

"You're lying."

"Okay, I was. Is it still alive?"

"Alive, yes. But my dick is tired so you aren't getting any. Take what I gave you."

He said that like, if I had been a dog, he tossed me a bone. My friend came out of the bathroom. The rejuvenated look on her face read she had been sated. Meanwhile, my pussy was still humming. I sucked my teeth, hopped up, and made my way to the bathroom. If I could have slammed the door, I would have. In my mind, I pictured him chuckling at my pain. Didn't matter. Me and Mr. Hitachi had a meeting in the bathroom.

It didn't take me and my electricity operated friend long to get me to that orgasm I wanted. Once done, I cleaned him up. Washed my hands and face and made my way back into the room. There was no Jaylin, only a shamefaced, but thoroughly satisfied friend.

I crawled back on my bed as she sat on hers.

"You want to talk about what all that was about?" I asked just to put her on the spot.

"No."

"Can we talk about why he said he was playing to win?"

She chuckled lightly. "That was only his arrogance."

"Or was that some unfinished business between you two?"

She took a deep breath then exhaled hard. Ran a hand through her disheveled hair and adjusted her loosely hanging night shirt. For a moment, she just looked at me, and for a fleeting second, there was something else that skittered across her face that I couldn't read. But it was gone just as quickly.

Then she smiled at me. "That was about you getting your story. Now you can tell the world what happened between Jaylin, you and I, *If Only for Another Night*."

FATE
Kalima Shahada

The doorbell chimed and I rushed to the door. Having an idea as to who it was, I stopped to look in the mirror. I took my hand and combed some misconstrued curls back into place. My hair hung on my shoulders. I checked my lips; my gloss was still glistening. My breasts sat up just right, and my long skirt hugged my curvy hips.

I must say that a lot of things had changed in a few months. I dropped a few pounds, my face no longer showed any signs of distress, and my eyes were no longer puffy and red. At the age of 30, I looked good, despite being depressed for months. I found out my husband had been cheating on me, over ten months ago. He moved out and I haven't seen him since. Now, he stood outside my door with his son he'd had during our marriage. Saying I was nervous was an understatement. Was I crazy for picking up the phone when he called to announce his new bundle of joy had arrived? Was I crazy for inviting them over? Some would say, yes. However, my views about marriage changed after I met the one and only, Jaylin Jerome Rogers. Thinking back to the day I met him was therapeutic among many other things.

That day, I looked out into the nocturnal sky and down at the ocean. As the water washed ashore onto my feet, I wiped my tears and vowed that I was no longer looking into the past, but into the future. I took a final gaze at the ocean then stood up. My wedding ring was still on my finger, so I pulled it off and tossed it into the water. I knew now that solidified my decision to move forward rather than backwards. I turned around and was startled, as I stared into the most beautiful eyes.

"I'm sorry for startling you," he said in a soothing tone. "I heard you over here crying, so I came to see what was up."

I shook my head from side to side. I had to have been dreaming, because guys this good looking didn't exist in real life. I scanned my eyes from the top of his head, down to his big feet. He had short curly hair. His gray eyes were the most beautiful I'd ever seen. His goatee was trimmed nice and neat. I couldn't believe how smooth and tanned his caramelized skin looked; it was flawless. He wore pants that looked tailored specifically for him, and his shirt had a few buttons undone at the top, exposing his muscular chest.

"Are you okay?" he asked again. I could see the compassion in his eyes.

The sound of his masculine voice knocked me out of my daze. I couldn't believe this complete stranger had me so mesmerized. This was definitely a first. I exhaled and finally spoke.

"I'll be fine, once I make it home."

I made an attempt to walk past him. I had to get away from him, because I didn't want him to notice the lust in my eyes. I have never, and I mean ever, got this excited from just a glance. It felt like a puddle was forming in my panties.

"Wait," he said then grabbed my hand. "Where do you live?"

I looked at him strangely, and he quickly let my hand go. "Why?"

"Because I'd like to walk you home. You shouldn't be walking out here on this beach all alone at night?"

"Why do you care?" I asked with an attitude. I then placed my hands on my hips. "What are you, the beach patrol?"

He shot me a serious gaze. "No, but I know there are dangerous people out here in the world. A beautiful young lady, such as yourself, shouldn't be out here alone."

I wanted to smile when he moved my blowing hair away from my face and called me beautiful. But I had been deceived before and had to stay firm.

"What makes you think I should trust you? How do I know you're not one of those dangerous people out here, trying to hurt me?"

He moved closer to me. So close that he towered over me. I could smell the cologne he wore. Better yet, I could smell his aftershave, and the body soap he used. I never smelled a man this scrumptious before. He was a stallion. He stood firm like a warrior. He was so fine that he took every ounce of my breath away.

"Baby, I have no desires to hurt you," he said endearingly as he stared directly into my brown eyes. It felt like he was staring into my soul. "The bottom line is I'm a caring man. I wouldn't feel right, if I didn't see to it that you got home safely."

I continued to put up a fuss, even though I loved the attention he gave me. "I don't know you. You could be some psycho for all I know."

This time, he shook his head and chuckled. And even though I was serious, I laughed too. I highly doubted that he was a psycho, but I was uncertain. His face looked like it could've been in magazines, not on the FBI's Most Wanted list. Hell! He looked like he should've been on a throne, with servants waiting on him hand and foot. A king was more like it.

Finally, he extended his hand and made an introduction. "I'm Jaylin. Jaylin Rogers. And you are?"

Eager to fuck you. That's what I wanted to say, but I just stood there, staring at his awaiting hand. When I didn't say anything, he grinned and showed his perfect white teeth. I cleared my throat, trying hard to gather myself.

"A . . . Amaya," I said barely audible.

"Amaya, nice to meet you."

The way he said my name in his deep baritone voice sent chills up my spine. I reluctantly linked my hand with his. His grip was so firm and strong, but his hand was soft as a baby's bottom.

"It's nice to meet you also."

"Since we're no longer strangers, allow me to walk you home. Feel free to tell me what's on your mind. I'm a good listener and I do offer great advice."

He seemed genuine and harmless, so I apprehensively agreed to walk to my house with him. For some odd reason, I felt safe in his presence. Minutes into our walk, a gust of wind came in, sending chills all over my body that was barely covered in a bikini. He saw me shivering and offered the shirt right off his back. Before I could protest, his shirt was off and wrapped around my shoulders. I couldn't believe my eyes. His body was ripped from every angle. All of a sudden, I was no longer cold, but hot as hell. So hot, that I began to sweat. He held me close to him and that made me even hotter. We made small talk, and during our conversation, he said that he lived on the beach, a few houses away from where we were.

"So," Jaylin said as we continued walking toward my residence. "Why were you out here alone at night, crying? You're talking about everything else but that."

I sighed deeply. "Today is my eleventh year anniversary."

He shrugged and shot me a puzzled look. "What's wrong with that?"

Sadness washed across me. "As you can see, I'm spending it alone. My husband and I have been separated for seven months now."

"I'm sorry to hear that," he said compassionately.

"I caught him cheating on me," I continued. "He was with a chick he met prior to me, and proclaimed that he had ceased all contact with her, once we were married. Come to find out, they never stopped seeing each other. He insisted that was the first time they got together, since we became married. Then he said it was a mistake." I paused to take a deep breath. This revelation was beginning to upset me all over again. I thought I was past being upset, depressed and crying over my failed marriage. Obviously, I wasn't. This situation had been nothing but a nightmare, ever since it happened.

Jaylin seemed quiet and in deep thought when I was talking. Then he spoke up. "Did you believe him?" I looked into his eyes, as he awaited my answer. His question came as a surprise to me and I was trying to get my thoughts together. Since I hadn't responded, he questioned me again. "Did you believe him when he said it was a mistake?"

I lowered my head as I felt tears threatening to show up. "No, but when I looked into his eyes, I saw so much compassion and sorrow. I wanted to believe him. I wanted to believe he would never hurt me intentionally like he did. But I couldn't trust his word."

"Why couldn't you?"

"How could I when I found out she's pregnant?" Unable to control what I was feeling inside, I burst out crying. "She's pregnant with MY husband's child. I couldn't even give him a child, but the first time he cheated, he wound up giving someone the baby I prayed for. How could a baby be a mistake?"

No one understood the immense pain I was in. Being married to my husband for over a decade, and never getting pregnant, was very hurtful. I was depressed. For years it took a toll on me emotionally and mentally. To have my husband bring a child into this world, and I wasn't the mother, was gut wrenching.

I saw Jaylin swallow a huge lump that had formed in his throat. He pulled me closer to him and wiped my tears. "First, let me say to you that babies are not mistakes. A mistake is defined as an action or judgment that is misguided or wrong. What your husband did to you may have been wrong, but the baby is just a result of his actions. Sometimes, actions have serious consequences. Consequences that can always be worked through, depending on how the parties involved handle it. Has he tried to reconcile?"

"Yes. He calls me every day, telling me how sorry he is. I know he's remorseful—well, I would like to think he is, but—"

"But what?"

"It's complicated. I have thought about forgiving him and trying to patch up my marriage. The second I think about that possibility, I quickly realize how stupid and desperate I would look if I forgave my husband who cheated on me and got another woman pregnant."

Jaylin sighed and narrowed his eyes to look at me. I thought I saw a hint of frustration. "Who gives a damn about what other people think? Them motherfuckers aren't paying your bills, are they? They're not walking in your shoes every day, and they do not know the details revolving around your marriage. Listen, sweetheart. It's not about how others see you. It's about how you feel in your heart. Do you still love him?"

I wiped the tears that had streamed heavily down my face. "Of course I do. He was my everything."

"Do you think you would've been able to forgive him, if she hadn't gotten pregnant?"

"I truly don't know. The pregnancy has been weighing heavily on my mind, and when I think about the actual act, it angers me. It makes me wonder was it me? Could I have done something to make him stay faithful? What was so wrong with me? I've racked my brain with a million questions, wondering what I did to make him seek another woman."

This time, I cried uncontrollably. Jaylin held me in his arms and continued wiping my tears. I was an emotional wreck, and had been since the separation. When I married my husband, I couldn't fathom being without him. I married him for richer or poorer, and for better or worse. I figured that if and when the worse came, we would've been able to toughen it out because we loved each other immensely. Never did I think the guy I was going to be with forever would hurt me to such degrees. He was my first, and I figured he was going to be my last.

"Look. Stop blaming yourself," he demanded. "I can tell that you have a lot going on for yourself, so don't you ever think it's your fault. The problem is with him, not you. Believe me when I say it's with him."

We were just five minutes away from my house when the sky turned an ugly gray. Thunder roared and it started pouring down raining. Within seconds, it started raining harder. The wind picked up and lightning came bolting from the sky. We started to run, but when I lagged behind, Jaylin swooped me up in his arms and took off running toward the direction I told him to go. I felt like Whitney Houston in the *Bodyguard* when Kevin Costner picked her up and carried her off stage while she was performing. He was her protector, and at that moment, I felt Jaylin was the same to me.

We made it to my home in no time, but not before we got drenched. We were soak and wet, but he didn't put me down until we were in the foyer of my house.

"I can't thank you enough," I said as I closed and locked the door. "I didn't mean to be a damsel in distress, but I seriously enjoyed your company."

I couldn't keep my eyes off of him. He looked even sexier dripping wet. My eyes roamed down below, and I couldn't help but to notice the bulge in his pants. Being that he was wet, I could tell he was packing. And I wasn't referring to groceries. I observed him as his eyes roamed my wet body as well. I saw his eyes light up at the sight of my huge breasts. I figured my nipples must've been hard, and by me being wet, I know it only magnified them. He stroked the hair on his chin while sucking his teeth.

"I'm glad that you got home safely," he said. "But I must get going. Good luck to you and your husband. I'm sure the two of you will work things out."

He made a move for the door. "Wait," I called after him. "You don't have to leave. The weather is pretty bad."

"I know, but I need to jet."

"You were kind enough to see to it that I made it home safely, now all I want is the same for you. Going out in that weather is not a guarantee you'll get home safely. At least, stay and wait out the storm."

He smiled and caressed the side of my face. His touch sent chills to my already cold body.

"I'll be fine."

The second he stepped one foot outside the door, lightning shot from the sky followed by loud thunder. It was so loud that it made my house rock. I heard car alarms going off in the distance.

"Please stay," I pleaded with my eyes, as he looked back at me.

When he stepped back inside my house, lightning flashed again as thunder roared ferociously. This one was more powerful than the one before. It felt like the whole earth shook. It scared me so much that I jumped into Jaylin's arms. At that moment, everything went pitch black. Jaylin looked outside, and it was also pitch black out there. He assured me it was going to be okay, and then he asked if I had any candles and a towel for him to dry off.

We maneuvered around in the darkness, until I was able to find some candles. The ones I found had illuminated the place just enough. As we both dried ourselves with towels, I couldn't thank him enough. If he hadn't been here, I would've been scared out of my mind. It wasn't because of the darkness alone. It was a combination of that and the weather outside. It seemed like it was a hurricane, tornado and storm, all rolled into one. The wind was blowing severely, the rain was pouring heavily, the lightning was flashing brightly and the thunder was so loud. The craziest thing, the meteorologists hadn't predicted it.

We were camped out in the living room. I was sitting on the sofa and he was sitting on the loveseat right across from me. We were out of our wet clothes. I was wearing a long ankle length, white satin lounging shirt. I gave him the only thing he could fit, which was my husband's robe that must've slipped through the cracks when I was throwing away everything that reminded me of him. I must admit that Jaylin made the robe look good. I was upset, because I didn't have any food to offer him—food that didn't need to be cooked. However, when I mentioned that I had a bar downstairs, he asked me to lead the way. He scanned the selection while holding a candle, and quickly pulled out a bottle of Remy. I grabbed two glasses and we settled back into the living room, under the aura of the candlelight. I turned on an old radio I found, that only needed batteries to operate. I found a station that was playing slow songs. After downing two glasses of the alcohol, I became a little tipsy. After all, I didn't drink, but under the circumstances I was willing to do anything to alleviate the pain.

"You never told me why you were strolling the beach at midnight," I said.

"I couldn't sleep."

"Why? What's your story?"

He didn't hesitate to answer. "I'll just say that my story is not much different than yours."

I sat shocked, while he revealed his reason for not always being able to rest peacefully at night. Jaylin had a lot going on, and sometimes, he didn't like being alone. Today marked a year since he'd been divorced from his wife. When he disclosed why she left him, I was flabbergasted. I was stunned to find out our situations were almost identical. He'd cheated on his wife with a former lover, and she became pregnant with their child. He confessed that he still loved his ex-wife dearly, but said that the two of them were better off today. I could sense that the whole ordeal had taken a toll on him, just as my situation had taken one on me.

I got up from the sofa and sat beside him on the loveseat. "I'm sorry," I said compassionately as I hugged him. Moments later, I broke away from the embrace. "Why did you do it?" I questioned as I turned his face toward me. "Why do men cheat when they say they love you?"

He released a deep breath. "I can't speak for other men, but I'm willing to admit that I fucked up. I'm not perfect, and everyone knows, especially my wife, that I will always love her."

"You referred to her as your wife. Do you always do that, even though the two of you are divorced?" I thought that was kind of peculiar, especially since they'd been divorced for a year.

"She'll always be my wife. I don't care if she marries someone else one, five, ten or twenty years from now. No other woman has had my heart quite like she has. It definitely belongs to her."

"What about the other woman?" I was curious to know how he felt about her. My husband said the woman he cheated with didn't mean anything. I was still trying to figure out if that was good or bad. "Do you love her too?"

"Yes, I do love her. She has my son and we've been through a lot. But I'm not in love with her, like I am in love with my wife. Basically, there is no comparison, even though many people believe there is."

I got so angry. He sounded just like my husband about how much he loved me, but yet still cheated.

"You mentioned the definition of a mistake. If you know it's a mistake, then why go there to begin with?" I had to get clarity, even though I highly doubted I'd understand how men operated.

"I cheated with the notion that she'd never find out, and it wasn't my intentions to hurt her. I do deeply regret how much I hurt my wife; however, by no means do I regret my son. He was a blessing to me, not a mistake. It took a while for her to accept him, but she now loves him as if he were her own. Sometimes, you have to realize that you can't go back and change things. All you can do is figure out the best way forward."

"That's going to be very difficult for me to do. To me, the child would be an everyday reminder of your infidelity. How is she able to deal with that?"

"It wasn't easy, trust me. But Nokea is a special kind of woman. That's why I love her so much. She would never take my indiscretion and use it as a reason to dislike my child. He's innocent in all of this. Her love for me guarantees much love for him. As for ending our marriage, she did what she saw fit. I couldn't fight that, no matter how hard I tried."

I swallowed hard, as the feeling of me possibly accepting my husband's child he fathered outside of our marriage, almost suffocated me.

"As for your situation," he continued on. "I'll ask you what I asked her in the beginning, because you never know what you're capable of doing until you try. Why get married if you're willing to throw in the towel after just one affair? Why get married if you're not willing to go through the storm and fight for your marriage? Why get married—"

Tears streamed from my eyes. "Why get married if you couldn't forsake all others?"

He held out his hands, defending his actions. "Sometimes, shit happens. No one can predict the future and our lives are so unpredictable. You know, deep in your heart, if your husband is capable of doing right by you. You're the one who knows if he can really make things right and not put you back on this path again. I don't have all of the answers. All I can do is tell you how it all turned out for me. We all know that men do stupid shit in the heat of passion, or without thinking logically, but many of us are not out to hurt the ones we love. I suggest that you hear your husband out and consider giving him another chance, if he deserves it. Again, you're the one who knows that better than me."

Jaylin reached out to wipe my tears. I felt a little better, but this was so hard for me because I was still deeply in love with my husband. I wanted us to reconcile our differences, but in no way was I there yet, like his *wife* appeared to be.

"I . . . I guess I could try." He smiled from my response. "If you and your wife ever got back together, do you think you could be the husband you know she truly deserves?"

"Honestly, no," he answered without hesitation. "I realized, through all of this, that I could never settle down with one woman and do right by her. She knows that I can't, so we don't have to go around pretending and arguing anymore over something that will never be. But that's me. Your husband may not operate like I do, and you shouldn't compare him to other men, because he's his own man. Just because a man refuses to be with one woman, it doesn't make him a bad person. You've got to consider other things about him too; things that you must take into consideration before you make your decision."

I knew my husband was a good man, and I wanted to believe that he didn't do any of this to hurt me. Still, I just didn't know if he could forever be faithful.

"Most women are strong; however, we can be vulnerable as well. Men don't understand what infidelity does to our self-esteem. It knocks us off that pedestal we thought we were on. When a man cheats, we're left wondering what we could've done better, or been better at, that would've held his interest. We wonder what the other women have that we don't. We question and evaluate everything in our life, big or small, until we finally realize it wasn't us but the men in our lives. You say that losing your wife hurt, but can you imagine the pain she felt? It's a thousand times worse and it's how I feel right now. That's why I don't really know what I will ultimately do."

Jaylin put his arms around me, and I laid my head on his chest. Silence fell between us, as I felt peace and tranquility in this man's arms. I was so at ease; I never wanted to leave from them. My ears tuned into the radio. The song that bellowed from the speakers was a guy pleading to his lady to take him back after his affair. I assumed the song hit home for him because it hit home for me too.

I turned his face toward me, noticing a glassy look in his eyes. I guess this conversation may have been too much for him. It was too much for me too, and as we continued to sit in silence, I couldn't help but release more emotions. He continued to kiss my tears away, and when his lips descended upon mines, my heart almost stopped beating. His lips were so soft, as he kissed me tenderly. He kissed me deeper. When his tongue slipped into my mouth, my body heated instantly to a dangerous degree. My chest started palpitating, as my tongue did rotations in his mouth. We continued French kissing, and while his hand roamed underneath my long shirt, I immediately tensed up. He stroked my nipples until they were erect. It had been months since my last sexual encounter, but I couldn't believe the way my body was responding to a stranger. It felt like he was waking my body up from a coma; it never felt like this. My body clearly wanted . . . needed this man, and it wasn't taking no for an answer. Who was I to tell it otherwise?

"Why are you taking advantage of me?" I asked in a soft whisper.

"That's not what I'm doing, but if you want me to stop, just tell me and I will. All I want to do is take away some of this pain." He spoke breathlessly between kisses.

"No. Please don't stop," I moaned. "I need this, and I want the pain to stop, even if it's only for one night."

With that being said, he didn't stop. He laid me down on the sofa and kissed me intensively. I quickly untied the sash on his robe, which exposed his rippled chest. I closed my eyes and rubbed my hands up and down his chest. His chest was so chiseled. He kissed a trail from my lips all the way to my neck. He didn't leave one single area of my neck untouched, before he moved further down. He pulled off my shirt and freed my triple D's. He palmed my breasts that looked like two cantaloupes in his hand. He stared at them in amazement before he kneeled down. His tongue made contact with my nipple and I wanted to scream. He sucked, licked, and bit my nipples with so much precision that I did scream. It wasn't a scream of pain, but total pleasure.

As we both were naked, I lay mesmerized by his body. There was certainly nothing quite like it. He was so strong. He had muscles protruding from everywhere. With a body like that, I figured he had to exercise every day, maybe even twice a day. His body wasn't the only thing that had me mesmerized. I couldn't keep my eyes off of his nine-and-a-half inches of wonderfulness between his legs. I must say that it looked good enough to have for breakfast, lunch, dinner, brunch, snack, dessert and Taco Bell's fourth meal. Besides my husband, I never wanted a man so much before in my life. He stared into my eyes for any signs of protest, before inserting himself. When I didn't give him any gripe, he went for it. He felt so good inside of me that I wanted to cry. When I came, he aggressively picked me up and pinned me on the wall near the sliding glass door. With my legs wrapped around his waist, and my arms around his neck, he looked into my eyes with so much lust and kissed me feverishly. The heat that was radiating off of our bodies, I just knew it was going to set off the smoke detector. Even though the rained poured heavily, and the thunder intensified, the weather outside was no match for the explosion we were causing inside. We were brewing up our own category 10 hurricane. He ignited a fire in me that I knew even the firefighters wouldn't be able to put out. Within minutes, our bodies exploded and I started shivering like I was having a seizure. I yelled out his name so loudly, it could be heard for miles. Maybe even the people in the surrounding states heard me. His body trembled too, as we slid down the wall in ecstasy together.

In retrospect, I solely believed that things happened for a reason. God brought people into your life for a reason. It was fate that brought Jaylin to me that night on the beach. He knew that we needed each other in more ways than one. He helped me understand why men cheat and the reasoning behind it. He gave me insight of how men think, but made me aware that they're all very different. I helped him understand a women's pain, after her heart has been broken, due to a husband's infidelity. In just a few hours, we cleansed each other's mind, soul and definitely body. Upon meeting Jaylin, I was on the verge of a mental breakdown. I was depressed, and I cried several times a day, wondering what I could've done better. When he left the next morning, it was almost like I was cured. I no longer felt somber, instead I felt lively. I hadn't cried since that night, and I no longer asked myself, what I could have done better.

Instead, I asked God to guide me every day. I felt like I had a new lease on life, and I thanked Jaylin Jerome Rogers for that. I wanted to tell him that, but I haven't seen nor talked to him since that night. I didn't know where he lived, and I didn't want to seem like a stalker if I looked him up by his name. I decided to leave well enough alone. I figured we served our purpose for each other, just that one night.

The doorbell ringing again snapped me out of my daze. I sighed deeply as I prepared myself to see my husband, whom I haven't seen in months, and his newborn son for the first time. I turned the doorknob and a smile immediately etched across my face. Saying I was happy and shocked was an understatement.

"Jaylin?" I questioned as I felt my breathing intensify. Thinking back to the night when we'd had sex, it made my body temperature rise. I trembled and tingled in all the right places.

"What's up," he said. His eyes roamed all over me. "You look fine as ever."

Before I could utter another word, he rushed in, grabbed my face and kissed me like there was no tomorrow. When his tongue entered my mouth, my body felt like it had engulfed into flames. After all of these months, he still triggered something in my body that no one ever had. He had my hormones jumping sporadically. My body needed this man, and it needed him now. We kissed all the way into the living room. He led me to the same sofa he had me on months ago. He lifted my dress over my head and eased my panties down. I removed his jacket and anxiously unbuttoned his shirt. I couldn't wait to rub my hands down his chest. After I did just that, I moved down to the main attraction. I unzipped his pants, and he stepped out of them. I quickly freed his dick from his boxers. It looked so beautiful; it felt like I was looking at it for the first time. The way I was staring at it you would've thought I was holding the antidote to cure cancer. He laid me down, and my body trembled with anticipation. Before he entered me, I heard . . .

"Amaya!"

My body froze up. That wasn't Jaylin calling my name. I cautiously looked to the side, and saw my husband with an irate look locked on his face. He held a car seat in his hand that occupied his sleeping son. *Damn!* I thought. Now, I was the one who had some explaining to do. Jaylin was right. Life was so unpredictable.

LEAVE THE PANTIES AT HOME

Tiffani Warren

To say I was nervous would be an understatement. My eyes shifted to the clock on the wall, and for the last several hours, I hadn't heard one single word my business partners had said to me. With my legs crossed, I kept nodding and agreeing with what they were saying, but there was only one thing that consumed mind. Meeting Jaylin Rogers. I visualized what he would look like in person, even though I'd seen many pictures of him before. Through reading every single book in the Naughty Series, I had a clear picture of him sketched in my head. I wondered what he'd wear today, and all I kept thinking about was seeing those addictive eyes.

I wasn't the least bit worried about him liking me, because I was a beautiful, educated woman with curves at my hips that drove most men insane. My hair was almost all cut off, but I kept it trimmed and neat. When Jaylin reached out to me on Facebook, I wasn't surprised. We clicked immediately and checked in with each other almost every day. Then, one day, he asked if we could meet.

Normally, I wouldn't hook up with anyone I met on the internet. But after watching Jaylin's interaction with women online, I kind of felt as if I'd gotten to know him. I mean, there were moments that made me kind of skeptical about him, and some of the things he injected in his comments were rather jaw-dropping. For now, I pushed all of that aside and decided to get up close and personal with the man behind all of this madness. Some women loved him, others hated him. Men were trying to figure out what in the hell Jaylin had been drinking to get so many women, and some were simply jealous. Then there were those who insisted that you had to meet him in the flesh, in order to know the real deal.

The meeting wrapped up and the limo took me to the Four Seasons Hotel in NYC. Jaylin told me that he had reserved the penthouse suite that overlooked Manhattan. I made my way to it, looking dynamite in a white, short jumper outfit. A gold belt was secured around my tiny waist, and my model-like brown legs were on display. They looked as if I'd dipped them in baby oil. I sucked in a deep breath before knocking on the door and discovering what awaited me. Seconds later, the door clicked and squeaked open, yet no one was there.

"Hello," I said, walking inside and seeing no one in sight. "Is anyone here?"

As I turned the corner, I spotted Jaylin dressed in a navy, cheap-looking suit with a royal blue wife beater underneath it. The curls on his head appeared nappy to me, and from my view, those gray eyes that I awaited were dark brown and bloodshot red. He looked high, and the smell of marijuana filling the air, pretty much confirmed that he was. At about five-six or seven, he stood by the tall glass windows, staring outside as if he were in thought. A glass was in his hand, and he sipped from it, before clearing his throat and damn near choking.

"Excuse me," he said, holding up one finger and coughing. Coughed so hard that he looked to be foaming at the mouth. Specks of spit sprayed from his mouth, causing him to pound his chest and clear his throat again. I wasn't sure if I should help him or not, but by the time I got my thoughts together, he seemed okay. The signature goatee that I'd seen in pictures was more like a rugged beard that was in no way trimmed. He had the nerve to stand there and scratch it, like a dog with fleas.

"You know you're late, don't you?" he said.

I looked at my watch, not realizing that time had gotten away from me. It was only fifteen minutes past our meeting time. "For some reason, the limo driver went out of the way. But the good thing is that I'm here."

I guess he didn't like my answer because there was no reply. He placed the glass on the table and walked up to me. I got a whiff of his strong cologne. What it told me was to keep my panties on! That shit stunk.

"Why don't you take a load off and have a seat," he said. "Or if you'd like, I can get you something to drink."

I had high hopes about seeing Jaylin, but things were going downhill. Fast. During our Facebook conversations, he seemed like he had his shit together. I kicked my girlfriends to the curb this weekend, just to be here with him. Thus far, I wasn't sure if I'd made the right move, and I started planning for an escape.

For now, though, I took his advice and sat on the L-shaped sofa. Told him that gin and a little juice would suit me fine. He went over to the tiny bar to make my drink. Once he was done, he brought the drink over to me, but tripped over a shaggy rug that lay on the hardwood floor. He stumbled, but managed not to spill my drink.

"Damn rug," he said, kicking it, as if the rug was the clumsy one.

"Be careful," I said, reaching for my drink. "You don't want to spill it, nor do you want to fall and injure your handsome face."

He rubbed the hair on his face and smiled. "You're right. I definitely don't want to mess up my face."

Maybe a fall would help it, I thought. I tried to be nice, and kept smiling, even though I was annoyed. Jaylin sat in a chair next to the couch. He kicked off his shoes that looked overly worn and had scuff marks all over them. Whatever happened to the black, square-toed leather shoes he often sported? In addition to that, the odor coming from his feet damn near knocked me out. I fanned the space in front of me and scooted down several inches on the couch.

"So," he said, adjusting his plastic watch that damn sure was no Rolex. He looked at the time again, and then lifted his head to look at me. "What are the plans for today? I'm the one visiting your city, and I assume we're not going to stay cooped up in this penthouse all weekend, are we?"

Truthfully, I was too embarrassed to go anywhere with him. I didn't want to be seen with him, especially since I'd bragged to all of my girlfriends about finally meeting the man of so many women's dreams. Chile, if they only knew.

"You know what, Jaylin. I don't want to go out and paint the town. What I'd rather do is just chill with you, talk and listen to some music. That's unless you're hungry. If you are, we can go downstairs to get a bite to eat, or feel free to order something through room service."

"I may have to do that later, but I don't want to break you, since you're paying for this room and everything. I must say that it's real nice. You definitely have good taste."

"I sure do, but I don't recall offering to pay for your room and meals. With all of the money that you have, why would you expect for me to?"

He leaned forward and rubbed his ashy hands together. "Well, you see, money is a little tight these days. Child support be kicking my ass and pussy don't always come free. I can pay you back, once this deal I've been working on comes through."

"Sorry, but you may as well check out of here right now, if you can't afford this room. How in the heck did you get in this penthouse anyway, without paying for it upfront?"

Just then, I heard his cellphone ring. He reached into his pocket and pulled out a Jitterbug flip-phone that looked like it had been dropped a million times. I sat quietly and shook my head.

"Yeah, nigga, I'm glad you called," he shouted into the phone. As he smiled, I got a glimpse of his stained teeth. Pearly whites my ass. Then, he had the nerve to pick at his nose. I held my breath, hoping that he wouldn't find a booger. Thankfully he didn't, but he kept wiggling his nose in search of one. "I'm entertaining this li'l shorty right now, so I'll hit you back in about an hour." His eyes zoned in on my cleavage and he licked across his dry lips. "Nah, maybe two hours for sure. I may be busy."

Within the hour, there was no question that I'd be gone. Jaylin finished his conversation and propped his feet on the glass table. He lifted the glass he sipped from and swirled around the brown liquid inside.

"As I was saying, I got the room covered if you don't, so don't worry about it. And before I forget," he said. "It's good to finally meet you. I didn't think you'd look this damn sexy, especially from looking at your pictures on Facebook that weren't so attractive. For a minute, you had me worried. I saw that picture with you in sandals and a purple dress. I was like . . . where in the fuck did she get that dress from? Dollar General?"

Really? I wanted to go off on this fool, but decided not to. If anything, seeing him was such a letdown. I had concocted a plan in my head to use the bathroom and call one of my friends. She'd say it was an emergency, and then I could get the hell out of here. Since I hadn't said much, Jaylin came over to the couch and sat next to me. He was pretty close, making me real uncomfortable. I had a chance to see him close up. The holes in his skin, and the heavy makeup that covered them, made this fool look casket ready. Blackheads could be seen for days, and that awful smell on him was burning my nostrils. I couldn't help but to inquire.

"I don't mean no harm, but what is that smell? Is that your breath, Jaylin? Please tell me it isn't."

He blew his breath at his hand and sniffed it. "I don't know. It ain't me, but I smell something too. Kind of smell like a woman on her rag or something."

He slapped his leg and laughed. Okay. This was it for me. I moved away from him again and released a deep sigh.

"Look, Mr. Rogers. I must be honest and tell you how disappointed I am in seeing you like this. Those pictures you sent me, and the way you're described in those books, it— you look nothing like that."

He cocked his head back and frowned. "So, what you trying to say? That I'm ugly or something?"

"What I'm saying is you look nothing like I thought you would look."

"Well, that's too bad, because you look exactly how I thought you would look. I can't wait to eat you, and you should have left the panties at home. Maybe when I toss this nine-plus inches your way, you'll see that I'm the real deal."

He shot up from his seat, trying to prove his point. The first thing I saw was a big-ass hole in the center of his dingy drawers and his sacks hanging. I thought I saw an itsy-bitsy dingaling, but with an embarrassed look on his face, he pulled his pants back up.

"Wait until it gets hard," he said, pointing to his *stuff*. "When it does, this a bad boy right here."

I hopped up and was so done with this. I had truly had enough. I should've left when I saw that his shoes had holes on the bottom. But I tried to give him the benefit of the doubt.

"I think I'd better go," I said with a fake smile. "Don't let me waste anymore of your time or mine."

I tucked my purse underneath my arm and moved toward the door. Jaylin reached out to grab my arm and he yanked it so hard that I stumbled.

"Bitch, you don't walk until I say walk! You don't move unless I tell you to move. You don't speak unless I want you to and you don't complain when I'm in the process of trying to give you something."

Now, that sounded a little like Jaylin, but it was still a bit much. I tried to snatch away from him, but before I knew it, he let go of my arm and backslapped me so hard that I hit the floor. I now regretted putting myself in this situation. If I made it out of this, I would never, ever meet up with anyone I'd met on Facebook.

I crawled on the floor and he squeezed me by the back of my neck to pull me up. He forced me against the couch and tried to pry my legs open with his.

"You strong, but damn sure not as strong as me," he shouted.

He ripped off his jacket and wife beater, exposing his chest. Nappy beads of hair covered it, and his potbelly poured over his belt. At that moment, I started to cry. What in the hell happened to his chiseled chest and solid abs?

Trying to fight back, I reached out to grab his hair. My fingers got tangled in that mess and thick grease covered them. Since I couldn't get my fingers out of his hair, he bit my wrist and slapped me one more time. I tumbled over the couch, and he came after me, roaring like a tiger. I kicked and screamed as he raised my skirt and yanked down my panties. After removing them, he plopped on top of me and threw my legs over his shoulders. He plunged his dick inside of me and my eyes shot wide open. Sadly, I didn't feel a thing but his razor-sharp hairs, grinding against me. I covered my face and screamed at the top of my lungs.

"Noooooooooo . . . !"

I jumped from my sleep with my heart racing. Beads of sweat covered my whole face and my body trembled. Even though it was a dream, I was scheduled to meet Jaylin tomorrow afternoon. I had a change of heart, so I tossed my covers aside and damn near slipped on the floor as I ran to my computer to reach out to him on Facebook. I figured he was on there being naughty, and sure enough he was. I sent a quick message to his inbox, telling him that something had come up and there was no need for him to travel to NYC tomorrow, unless he still had plans to visit a friend and handle some business. He responded with:

JAYLIN: WHY THE CHANGE OF PLANS?

ME: SORRY. THIS WAS UNEXPECTED.

JAYLIN: I WAS REALLY LOOKING FORWARD TO MEETING YOU.

ME: I KNOW. ME TOO.

JAYLIN: IF YOU WERE, THEN YOU KNOW WHAT YOU HAVE TO DO.

ME: I CAN'T GET AWAY. MAYBE NEXT TIME.

JAYLIN: SURE. IF ANYTHING CHANGES, LET ME KNOW. I STILL HAVE TO TRAVEL TO NYC FOR A MEETING, AND MY FRIEND, JAMES, IS LOOKING FORWARD TO MY VISIT. MY PLANE ARRIVES AT NOON.

ME: I'LL LET YOU KNOW IF ANYTHING CHANGES, BUT I'M ALMOST POSITIVE THAT I WON'T BE ABLE TO GET AWAY.

JAYLIN: CAN'T SAY I DIDN'T TRY. STAY SWEET, BABY. ALL LOVE.

I sighed from relief and shut down my computer. Throughout the night, I tossed and turned, thinking about that horrible dream. And for whatever reason, I remained curious about how Jaylin really looked. By morning, I decided to make my way to the airport, just so I could see if he was more like the man in my dreams or like the man I'd seen in pictures. I changed into a simple sundress and covered my eyes with dark sunglasses. Just so Jaylin wouldn't notice my short hair, I put on a straw hat. I was clearly in disguise, as I waited in the baggage claim area. His plane had just landed, and I expected for him to come for his luggage soon.

Almost twenty minutes later, I sat in a chair and got the shock of my life. It was him, and I knew so because several women were snapping their heads to the side and whispers were in full effect. One woman actually fell because she wasn't watching where she was going. No man on earth could strut through the airport like that but Jaylin. It was as if he was moving in slow motion, and the closer he got, everything about him was confirmed. I saw the curls, I witnessed the goatee and the signature diamond watch was surely glistening. There were no holes in those shoes, and many muscles ripped through his 6'2 frame. I was mad at myself for cancelling on him, but trying to correct myself, I tossed the hat aside and hurried to make my presence known. I rushed through the crowd, bumping a few shoulders and almost tripping my damn self. But before I reached Jaylin, I saw another woman walk up to him. Seeing her halted my steps, especially when I saw that she was all smiles and so was he. He kissed her cheek, and after he grabbed his luggage, they walked side-by-side together. Wondering who she was, I quickly reached for my phone and sent him a text message.

ME: HEY YOU. IT'S ME. CHANGE IN PLANS AGAIN. I'M ABLE TO PICK YOU UP FROM THE AIRPORT IN ABOUT THIRTY MINUTES. ARE YOU THERE? WOULD LOVE TO SEE YOU.

I followed closely behind him and his female companion. He halted his steps and removed his phone from his pocket. I could see him reply to my text, and when he proceeded to walk again, I assumed a reply message had been sent. My phone vibrated and I read the text.

JAYLIN: I'LL BE BUSY ALL DAY AND TOMORROW. NOT SURE IF I'LL HAVE TIME TO HOOK UP THIS TIME AROUND. MAYBE NEXT TIME.

I figured he was giving me a dose of my own medicine, but that was on me for letting this opportunity pass me by. He wasted no time hooking up with someone else, but too bad because I wasn't willing to give up so soon.

ME: FUNNY. I'M ALREADY AT THE AIRPORT AND I SAW THIS EXTREMELY ATTRACTIVE MAN THAT I WOULD LOVE TO DO SOME OF THE CREATIVE AND NAUGHTY THINGS WITH THAT WE DISCUSSED ON FACEBOOK. IF YOU TURN AROUND, YOU'LL SEE ME. IF YOU LIKE WHAT YOU SEE, ALL YOU HAVE TO DO IS SMILE.

I hit the send button. A few minutes later, Jaylin stopped again to read my text. He put his luggage on the floor and slowly turned around. He narrowed his eyes to look at me, and then turned right back around. No smile, no nothing. My heart fell to my stomach. My feelings were a little bruised too, until my phone vibrated again, alerting me that I had a text message. I hurried to read it.

JAYLIN: SEXY, JUST AS I HAD PREDICTED. BUT NO GAMES, BABY. IF I TELL YOU WHO I AM, YOU'D BETTER BELIEVE ME. LET ME SAY GOODBYE TO MY FRIEND AND I'LL HIT YOU UP IN ABOUT AN HOUR. TELL ME WHERE TO MEET YOU AND BE SURE TO LEAVE THE PANTIES AT HOME.

There was no need for him to demand it, especially when I had planned to do just that. Leave my panties at home—for sure.

To be continued . . .

Back Down Memory Lane Continued
Author Unknown

I was lying across my bed writing. My mind was consumed with material for my next novel and my pen was moving so fast that I thought I'd break it. I smiled at what I'd written. Laughed a little and also shook my head. These characters were a mess, and all of them had a serious place in my heart. As I paused to massage my hands, I heard footsteps coming down the hallway. I figured it was Jaylin, even though I hadn't seen him for the past several days. I hoped he wasn't coming back for a piece of his birthday cake, because I'd put a serious dent in it. The rest, I threw in the trash, just so I could avoid eating the whole thing by myself.

With a yellow, thigh-high shirt on, I turned to my side to look toward the doorway. Seconds passed before Jaylin appeared dressed to kill in rich black. The satin-like vest, and crisp, straight-collared shirt he rocked underneath, fit his frame like it was tailored to put his toned biceps on display. A thin black tie was around his neck and his black, shiny shoes were without one scuff. His diamond watch had a black-face too, and the leather belt around his pants fit his waistline to a capital T. With a fresh haircut, his lining was sharp as ever. Tinted shades shielded his eyes, but he removed them as he came further into the room.

"What you writing?" he asked then sat on the bed.

Instantly, I got a whiff of his cologne and was forced to keep my Naughty thoughts to myself. Knowing that lying on the bed with my ass in his view would get me in trouble, I quickly sat up and closed my spiral notebook.

"Nothing interesting," I said. "Just writing."

"Well, hurry up and get finished. Throw on some clothes and go with me. Also," he said, reaching into his vest. He pulled out the contract we had previously discussed and laid it on the bed in front of me. "I added a few clauses that may be beneficial to the both of us, but the contract is signed. So get busy on the next phase, Miss Author. I, as well as many others, have been waiting patiently for something else to pop off."

"I understand, but you already know how difficult it is for African American authors to get in with the folks in Hollywood. Trust me, I'm trying."

"Try harder."

I thanked Jaylin for signing the contract, but also inquired about where he wanted me to go with him.

"Time to go handle some business. I want you to holler at some potential investors, and it's important that you get to know as many as possible. I also need to seal the deal on a few things, and it's always a pleasure for me to have you around when I'm trying to get things done. You have a way with men, and your friendly smile, along with your personality, tends to warm their hearts. I just got off the phone with an investor in Jamaica, Mr. Tiles. He couldn't stop talking about you, and he expressed how much the others connected with you during your visit. That's a good thing, and it's time to roll internationally."

I smiled and thought about how well things had gone in Jamaica too. Jaylin had always put forth every effort to align me with the right people who could elevate me to the next level. He seriously didn't know how much I appreciated him. "Thank you" just didn't seem like it was enough.

I got off the bed and went into the walk-in closet. "I know we're going to handle some business, but exactly where will that be? I don't know what I should wear."

"We're going to a St. Louis Cardinals baseball game. Don't go putting on shorts and a T-shirt, because we'll be in the Premier Owner's Suite with some important people. Dress accordingly."

Jaylin left the room, and I remained in the closet, looking for something to wear. Truthfully, I was kind of laidback when it came to clothes. I didn't have a lot of brand-named items, as that kind of stuff didn't move me. Most of my clothes were pretty simple, like me. I figured I could jazz up any outfit with accessories, so I opted for a white linen fitted dress that cut above my knees and gripped my curves. Since it was sleeveless, I grabbed a short black jacket and accessorized the entire outfit with red, black and white accessories. I fluffed the curls in my long hair and put on my makeup like a work of art. Since I was going to a Cardinals game, I stepped into a pair of custom glittery pumps that had the Cardinals logo on it. They gave me much height, and I was quite pleased with my whole attire. Jaylin was too, and he complimented me as we headed for his car.

"That's what I'm talking about, baby. You rocking those shoes, but that ass sitting real pretty in that tight dress."

"Thanks. It's not tight, but fitted. And just for the record, you look pretty awesome too. Now, on another note, how did your little adventure go? Did you make time to meet new women?"

He nodded. "Yes, plenty of them. One at a club, several at hotels, one I already knew, and another I ran into at the beach. All very interesting women, but I'm not going to tell you specific details because yo ass will start writing another book."

I laughed. There was no secret that Jaylin knew me all too well.

We made our way to the Busch Stadium. I assumed it would be jam-packed and it was. The Cardinals fans were always out in full effect, and the second we hit Downtown St. Louis, that was pretty obvious. Traffic was at a standstill. Jaylin was always impatient, so he managed to maneuver in and out of traffic, trying to make his way to the reserved parking garage.

"Before we go inside," he said. "You already know what's up when dealing with the one percent in America who are uppity, but are always looking for ways to invest their money. Stay away from the ladies, I'll handle them. Besides, when they see you with me, they're not going to like you. Remember to flirt with your eyes, not with your mouth. Show interest in what they're doing and let them know that you got it going on too. They'll probably be Googling you when you walk away. Smile at the arrogance, and don't get caught rolling your eyes. Remember that the sloppiest dressed man is, most likely, a billionaire, so don't ignore him. And don't waste time conversing with the brothers in there, because many of them are too full of themselves, too cocky and too arrogant. We both already know that some black people ain't gon' do a damn thing for another. Lastly, when you shake hands with anyone, remember to tell them your name. It's how you brand yourself, and most people will remember that they met you."

"I get it, and I've heard it all before from you. I won't disagree with anything you've said, but please do not be peeking over shoulders tonight, watching me work my magic."

Jaylin swerved into a parking spot and shielded his eyes with the shades again. "I won't if you don't. Now, let's go increase our financial statuses."

We got out of the car and made our way inside to the elevator. Already, Jaylin was working it. He strutted through Busch Stadium like he'd paid for it in full. Everybody stopped to look at him as he walked by, and he shook hands with what seemed like some important people. The elevator took us up to the suite, and when the doors opened, he extended his hand to let me go first. Almost immediately, many heads turned in our direction. There was a mixture of people in business suits, to women who were scantily dressed. Some people had on Cardinals gear, while many others looked like they were about to sit at a boardroom table. I certainly didn't feel out of place, and neither did Jaylin. Even though we were in the minority, it didn't matter. The second several of the white men saw Jaylin, they were all over him. One brother sat on the couch with a "hater" look washed across his face. I could only shake my head and kept it moving in another direction. It wasn't long before I joined in on a conversation between two Caucasian men who were casually dressed.

"So, you're a writer," one of them asked.

"Yes. A national bestselling author, screenplay writer, producer . . ."

I went on to talk about the international work I was involved in, and both men appeared tuned in and impressed. They continued to question me about my credentials, and I also showed interests in their line of work as well. One man was the CEO of a pharmaceutical company, and the other was a retired multi-millionaire who used to work for Ford Motor Company. We talked about everything from cars to the CEO assisting me with moving some of his products overseas. Book publishing came up during the conversation, as well as ghostwriting. Everybody had a story to tell, even the wealthy property developer and film producer who had also joined in on the conversation. Somebody was definitely looking out for me, and it was no coincidence that these people had come into my life at the right time.

"Would you like something else to drink?" One of the men asked me.

"I do, but since I want to get another hotdog, I'll also get a refill. Thanks for asking, and can I get you something while I'm away?"

"No," he said, patting his belly. "I'm pretty full."

I nodded and excused myself from the gentlemen who included me in a very positive conversation. The moment I stepped away, I saw Jaylin talking to the same two men, but looking over one's shoulder. A grin was on his face and he delivered a slow nod toward me. He then lifted his glass and turned it up to his lips. Brown liquid was inside; I assumed it was Remy. To his left were three white chicks, one black. They were definitely seeking his attention, but the one thing I loved about Jaylin was he didn't get off into the groupie thing. He could sense a gold digger a mile away, but it never stopped them from trying. As he moved, they moved. One of the white chicks who could have been a professional cheerleader reached out to him. I watched as he leaned in close to listen to what she was saying. She held on tight to his bicep and flung her long hair aside to show her pretty face. It almost resembled Kim Kardashian's, but Kim had more curves on her hips. Jaylin smiled and seemed tuned in to the conversation, but the look on his face said it all. He was all about business, something that didn't appear to be included in her conversation. I saw him walk away and move on to converse with a man who looked slouchy. When I walked up to introduce myself, sure enough, he was the billionaire of the bunch. Surprisingly, he was down to earth and very knowledgeable about business. He tossed out plenty of advice to Jaylin on some of the property deals he had been pursuing in Detroit, Chicago, as well as in Miami. As for me, he gave me his business card so that we could further discuss my involvement in building up ports in third world countries. He confirmed that he was willing to invest.

I walked away from that conversation feeling good. Even stopped to converse with a few brothers who all had smiles on their faces. Jaylin had warned me, and after five minutes, all I listened to was a bunch of insults regarding our own people and bragging. "I got this . . . I own that. I drive a Mercedes, and my house is by the ocean. My kids are in private school, and these low-life niggas will never amount to nothing." All of that was followed by one of them trying to get some pussy. As he whispered close to my ear, Jaylin walked up and tugged at my arm.

"Aye," he said with a stern look on his face. "I want you to meet somebody over here." He looked at the man standing next to me and extended his hand. "Jaylin Rogers. Sorry to interrupt, but this is kind of important."

The man didn't bother to shake Jaylin's hand. All he did was shrug and walk away. I regretted that some of the more elite African Americans acted this way, and it was one of the reasons why the crabs-in-a-barrel effect was alive and going strong.

Jaylin leaned against the bar with his elbow on top of it, looking at me. "I thought I told you not to waste your time. You could have spent that thirty minutes talking to the gentlemen over there who I saw Googling your name."

I just shook my head, thinking about the one percent who were always in Jaylin's company. It made me appreciate my simple life even more. "I was just trying to be nice, even though he was attempting to do other things. As for the Googling thing, great. Nothing but positivity, and I don't mind them thinking that I'm the writer and producer who is actually worth forty-million dollars."

I laughed and walked away from Jaylin to go to the restroom. Right at the exit door stood those groupies who displayed fake smiles. I smiled back and kept it moving.

When I got to the restroom, I tinkled and washed my hands. The marble countertop was beautiful, as was the gold-like faucets. The whole place was spotless, smelled like strawberries, and soft white towels were neatly folded on a shelf. As I reached for one to wipe my hands, I heard the door open. I couldn't see who it was, but my heart dropped to my stomach when the lights went out.

"Candyman, candyman," Jaylin softly whispered. He knew how afraid I was to watch that movie, but I couldn't help but to laugh.

"Stop playing and turn the lights back on. Now, Jaylin, I'm not playing."

He flicked the lights back on then walked up to me with his hands in his pockets. A smile was on his face and we stood face-to-face in front of the marble countertop and mirror.

"Scary ass," he said. "I can't believe you're still scared of that mess."

"Well, believe it because I am. Now, what are you doing in the women's restroom?"

"I saw you come in here, and I wanted to tell you how sexy you look out there, working your so-called magic. Like always, I'm impressed. That kind of shit really turns me on."

"You should be impressed, and that's what you get for, sometimes, underestimating me. In case you forgot, I learned from the best."

I winked. Jaylin's smile grew because he knew I was referencing him. I turned to look in the mirror again, and as I started to slide more gloss across my lips, he stood behind me, watching.

"Candyman—"

I swung around and covered his mouth with my hand. "Please, stop. I'm serious, Jaylin. Do not say that shit while we're standing in front of this mirror."

He removed my hand and laughed. I seriously didn't see a damn thing funny, and I was ready to get the hell out of that restroom. But before I made a move, Jaylin walked over to the door and locked it. He flicked the lights off again and came up to me.

"I'm done playing," he said. "It's time to get serious. Where in the hell is my birthday present at?"

"You mean your belated birthday present, don't you? Wherever it's at, it's definitely not in this restroom."

"I think it is, and as a matter of fact, I know so."

Jaylin backed me up to the marble countertop and pressed himself against me. I felt his package swell, inch by inch. A part of me wanted to rip off his clothes and have at it. Then there was something that told my ass to run! For the moment, I couldn't. My feet felt like concrete had been poured over them. I stood, inhaling Jaylin's cologne and allowing him to plant a trail of delicate kisses along the side of my neck.

"Mmm," he moaned in a soft whisper. "You smell good. So good that I want you on this counter, right now, so I can taste you."

I sucked in a deep breath then slowly released it into the air. My eyes fluttered from his soft kisses against my neck, but when his lips touched mine, I backed away.

"Let's not go there, Jaylin. I . . . we are wrong for trying to travel down this road again, and I don't think it would be in our best interest."

"I don't quite understand what is wrong with two people who care about each other, deciding to have sex. And only I know what is in my best interest, not you. All I'm asking for is ten minutes. That's it."

"Ten minutes that—"

Jaylin silenced me when he reached up and held the sides of my face. Even in darkness, I could see those eyes staring into mine. "Stop talking about what we shouldn't be doing and let's just do it. If you don't have ten minutes, then give me five. I know I'm good for that, aren't I?"

I stood silent for a few seconds, thinking that maybe it was time for us to stop playing these games and just do it, like he'd said. Resisting him was getting me nowhere, and all it did was make me one horny bitch. In response to him, I leaned in to attack his lips. As the kiss intensified, so did our breathing. Jaylin lowered his hands to reach underneath my dress and massage my ass. We grinded against each other, leaving no breathing room in between us. I could feel pressure from his dick that had grown to full capacity. Wanting to see it, feel it and possibly taste it, I quickly reached for his belt buckle. Within seconds, his pants were unzipped too. His muscle plopped out long, rock hard and pretty as ever.

"That's what I'm talking about," he said. "Now, face the mirror and bend over for me."

I faced the mirror and felt his hands comforting my hips. He raised the dress over my curves and it gathered at my waist. Since we were only working with five . . . ten minutes, I suspected that he would slide my panties to the side then glide inside of me. But as he eased them down to my ankles, I stepped out of them. Jaylin strapped up and returned to his position behind me. I was ready for action and was bent over the counter with my legs spread wide. My eyes shut when I felt the smooth tip of his head brush at the entrance of my moist hole, but when a hard knock came at the door, my eyes shot wide open.

"Fuck," Jaylin said. "Ignore it."

I definitely wanted to, but I couldn't. The knocks got louder and louder, and the person who was anxious to come inside started speaking out.

"Please open the door!" she shouted. "I can't hold it!"

I stood and hurried to lower my dress. Jaylin fussed as he backed away from me and tucked his hardness away.

"See, that's what you get for talking so damn much. Time wasted, no doubt."

I didn't bother to reply to his comment, because the last thing I wanted was for the woman to go get security to unlock the door.

"I'm going to open the door," I whispered. "Go in one of the stalls . . ."

Jaylin walked right by me and flicked on the lights. He turned to me, before opening the door. "I hide from no one. Let's get this night over with, so we can go back to the condo and finish what we started." His eyes shifted to the floor. "Don't forget to pick up your panties."

My eyes shifted to my panties on the floor, and as soon as I snatched them up, the woman came inside. Her face fell flat when she saw Jaylin, but a smirk appeared as she rushed by me to use the toilet. I left the restroom, hoping that I wouldn't see her again.

The remainder of the evening was a little awkward. Jaylin and I didn't say much else to each other, yet we kept eyeing each other and smiling from afar, as if our little incident in the restroom had never happened. On the drive back to the condo, he spent most of his time on the phone following up with some of the potential investors he'd spoken to tonight. All within one week, he made plans to travel to Atlanta, New York, the Bahamas and then back to Detroit. I asked if he ever intended to slow down.

"Maybe one day I will, but for now there are too many opportunities being sent my way that I can't resist. Be sure to follow up on your leads too. And if they don't call you, call them."

I was sure to do so. When we got back to the condo, he headed for the spare room and I went into mine. He was back on the phone, doing his thing. I showered and changed into a comfortable cotton gown that felt soothing against my skin. I lay across my bed, picked up my notebook and started writing again. Minutes later, my eyelids got heavy so I laid my head on the notebook and closed my eyes.

I was knocked out, until I felt the mattress move. When I looked up, I saw Jaylin lying next to me in bed. He was without a shirt and a gray, plush towel was wrapped around his waist.

"Wake up," he said. "I couldn't sleep. Too much on my mind."

I sat up, groggy as ever. "Well, call somebody to talk to. I've been doing a lot of writing and haven't gotten much sleep. I was finally able to shut it down."

Jaylin held my notebook in his hand and flipped through several pages. "I read some of this already. You know I'm going to change some things around, but for the most part, you had me hooked."

He moved around me and sat with his back against the padded, wingback headboard that damn near touched the ceiling. I crawled between his legs and laid my head against his solid abs. I felt his dick on my upper chest, but it wasn't hard.

"You're hooked because, when I'm writing, I always have some good characters to work with. Now, what's on your mind and why are you up so late?"

Jaylin started to ramble on about all of his business deals. He had so much money that it was crazy—made it seem like all he had to do was snap his finger and money would fall like rain. It still didn't seem like enough for him, and I knew that one of the things he appreciated about me was, I never asked him for one dime. Whatever he gave me, he gave on his own free will. Besides, he didn't believe in giving handouts or loans to people he considered friends. He'd been burned too many times, so what he did was offer encouragement, advice and connections to business minded people who could help his friends prosper in their field. That, to me, was more than enough.

"Are you falling asleep?" he asked. "I know I don't hear yo ass snoring, do I?"

"Probably," I whispered in a soft tone. "All of this talk about business and money, sometimes, gets boring. But it's nice to mix business with a little pleasure. You think?"

I lifted my head and pecked at Jaylin's abs. "One. Two. Three," I said, counting his six-pack as I kissed each muscle. "Four, Five . . ."

When I reached six, I moved a few inches down and peeled the towel away from his waist. His dick stood at great heights. I moved it toward my mouth, but he stopped me by grabbing and holding his steel.

"I've been thinking a lot about what you said." He released his goods, and with a smirk on his face, he placed his hands behind his head. "Maybe we shouldn't go there. I love the way our friendship has evolved, and the last thing I would want is for you to fall in love with me again. That, as we both know, could mean serious trouble for me."

I had to laugh at Jaylin. He definitely knew how I reacted to his shenanigans in the past, but this was certainly a new day. "Yeah, you wouldn't want me to do all of those horrible things that I did to you in the past for screwing me over, but then again, some of the chicks you dated did way more crazy stuff to you than I did. The worst thing I ever did was put sugar in your gas tank."

Jaylin laughed, as he must've briefly reflected on our dispute that day. "That was not the worst thing you did. I guess you forgot about that time when you bleached my suits. Now, that really pissed me off."

I shook my head and dropped my jaw in disbelief. "Have you lost your mind? I wasn't the one who bleached your suits. Nokea did, when she found out you went out of town with Felicia. Remember?"

He snapped his finger and nodded. "That's right. I remember now, but nothing happened between us. Nokea thought we got our freak on, but when she found out the truth, she had to apologize for ruining my suits."

"Yeah, well, what can I say? You have had your share of angry women, trying to get back at you for the hurt you caused. I know exactly how Nokea felt, and if you don't mind me saying, I think the two of you should reconcile one day. Just give it some thought. The only reason I say that is because you're so much happier when the two of you are together, and she is one woman that you will never be able to leave in the past. You're wasting your time seeking comfort elsewhere, and as your dear friend, I'm only telling you the truth."

I waited for Jaylin to respond, but he didn't touch my comment. "Other than that," I said. "I'd have to say that Felicia was the most psychotic, then Scorpio. More than anything, I think she was the one who put you in check."

"Bullshit. In check my ass." Jaylin touched his limp dick. "See how quick my dick deflated after that comment? That's because it doesn't appreciate being in the presence of women who don't know what they're talking about. Nobody—let me repeat—nobody will ever put me in check."

I shrugged. "Maybe not, but you have your opinion and I have mine."

"You're right. Your opinion doesn't matter, mine does. With that, get away from my dick and come up here. Give me some time to mull over your friendly advice, but tell me how or why you think this friendship feels so good."

I sat next to him and laid my head on his shoulder. Like always, I expected him to ignore my advice and change the subject back to me and him.

I sat next to him and laid my head on his shoulder. "I would be happy to tell you, but since my opinion doesn't matter, I'll keep my mouth, as well as my legs, shut."

"For how long is the question."

We laughed, talked and enjoyed each other's company until the wee hours of the morning. And when I woke up at 8:20 AM, I lay next to him, watching him sleep and thinking about how interesting he was. I wanted people to get to know him, and while there was a lot of naughtiness about him, there was also an equal amount of good. Having so much more to write, I eased out of bed, trying not to wake him. I put on my robe and went into the study with my notebook. My words flowed on the paper like magic, and it came so easy for me when I wrote about numerous characters that all came from my own personal experiences. That, without a doubt, was what made my books so damn interesting, as well as addictive.

THE END

41259978R00089

Made in the USA
Middletown, DE
07 March 2017